DARING WES

Cover Design by T.E. Black Designs

DARING WES

USA TODAY BESTSELLING AUTHOR
JULES BARNARD

FRESH FICTION PUBLISHING
JULESBARNARDBOOKS.COM

CHAPTER ONE

W es kept his eyes focused on his golf club—and not on his ex-girlfriend two sections up at the driving range.

Okay, he'd been watching Kaylee the entire time. But dammit, what was she doing here? Until a few days ago, when she'd ambushed him in the club's pro shop, he hadn't seen Kaylee in four years.

Her hair was shorter now, and not the long, nearly black sheet of silk it had been in college. And despite her natural elegance, she was doing a fine job hacking it up on the driving range.

The same guy she'd been with a couple of days ago slid his hand to her firm, round ass, causing a pulse to pound behind Wes's temples. It had been years since he'd seen Kaylee, but she'd been *his* the last time he had.

Wes shoved his club into his golf bag, prepared to call it a day and get the hell out, but Kaylee glanced in his direction. Her gaze landed on him and her eyes widened as though she hadn't expected to see him there.

Wes owned Club Tahoe with his brothers. What kind of bullshit was this? Everyone knew finding him at the golf range was a given.

Kaylee said something to the man she was with and they headed toward Wes.

Fuck.

"Do you have a minute?" she asked as Wes packed up his clubs.

He sent her a tight smile. "I've gotta return to the pro shop." Seeing Kaylee with someone else was like a fork in the eye, and Wes was doing everything he could to keep it together.

The guy with Kaylee put his arm around her shoulders, and Wes's hands tightened into fists. "This'll just take a moment. Kaylee said you went to college together and that you're a professional golfer."

Wes sighed. Had it not been for *this girl* and the head games she'd played in college, he would be a professional golfer, tearing it up on the tour. "I'm a pro at the resort."

McDouche gave Wes a blank stare.

Obviously, the guy didn't know much about golf. There was a big difference between playing tournaments and giving lessons as a course pro.

"Anyway," McDouche said, "Kaylee says you're good." He looked down at Kaylee and grinned. "I'd love to get my fiancée some lessons. She's just learning and could use the help."

Fiancée... *Fiancée?* Wes leveled Kaylee a look, and she flinched.

He let out a slow breath. Was this some sick joke? His ex showed up out of nowhere at his family's resort—*his turf* —and brought a fiancé?

"You don't have to do it," Kaylee said in a rush.

Her fiancé frowned. "We talked about this, Kaylee. You need lessons if you're going to join me on the course in Fiji during our honeymoon."

"Yes, but"—she glanced at Wes hesitantly—"he's probably busy. I don't even know if Wes gives lessons."

"I give them," Wes heard himself say.

He'd lost his mind. The last thing he should do was give lessons to Kaylee. She'd screwed him over, and neither he nor his golf career had ever fully recovered.

When Kaylee broke up with Wes, he'd been in the middle of the most pivotal tournament of his life. He'd shoved the breakup on the back burner and put all his mental energy into making it onto the pro tour, convinced he could make things right with Kaylee once he got home. Only Wes had bombed during tryouts, and "later" never came. By the time he returned, Kaylee had wrapped up her classes and left town. Wes never saw or heard from her again.

Golf was a head sport. Without focus, your score could easily go from six under to six over and knock you out of the game. Kaylee breaking up with him during the tournament had messed up his mental energy, and he hadn't recovered since.

The sad coincidence in this little reunion four years later was that Wes was once again attempting to qualify for the tour. Running into his ex was either shit-poor luck—or just what he needed to regain his winning edge.

She'd dumped him coldly without a good reason, and the idea of trusting Kaylee left a sour taste in his mouth. But if he could find out why she'd hightailed it out of town all those years ago, it might help him build back his mental game and give him back the edge he'd lost. "I'm available Tuesday and Thursday afternoons from four to five."

"Excellent!" McDouche with the overly chiseled jaw grinned at Kaylee, who appeared wary. "Kaylee can take lessons while she plans our wedding. We're having it at the club. Beautiful place you got here."

She was getting married...*at his motherfucking resort?* Had she lost her mind?

Kaylee lifted her chin in a defiant manner Wes remembered all too well. "I've always loved Lake Tahoe. My parents still have their cabin here. That's where Eddy and I are staying."

Eddy glanced between Wes and Kaylee. "Is there a problem? If you're too busy to do the lessons, I can find someone else."

"I'll do them," Wes said, staring at Kaylee.

Wes didn't know why Kaylee was really here, but it was too much of a coincidence that she was, and he was going to make damn sure and find out why.

———

KAYLEE TUCKED her hair behind her ears and slowly made her way toward Wes, standing near the driving range and talking to another guy. Wes was in a red Club Tahoe golf shirt, his hand shoved into his pants pocket, stretching the fabric of his khakis and giving her a nice view of his rear. Kaylee's ex was as fit as he'd been in college—more so, because he was broader and a little more filled out now.

Her heart fluttered—had been a fluttering, spastic mess since she saw Wes last week after nearly four years. They'd parted on such crappy terms. This was her chance to make things right. Only Wes was holding a grudge based on his reaction to seeing her again. And that was a grudge she had to get past if she had any hope of finding closure.

Kaylee had come into the pro shop with Eddy last week to look for a lightweight jacket for the cooler mornings on the golf course. But as soon as she'd caught sight of Wes behind the counter, her heart had nearly given out. She'd planned for her wedding to take place at Club Tahoe because the resort was beautiful and she'd grown up coming to the lake. And because she needed to see Wes one last time before she married.

Kaylee had no idea Wes would actually be working at the club. He'd had big plans for a golf career. Plans that had consumed him—to the detriment of their relationship. She thought she'd have to hunt him down. Possibly reach out to his father. But a few days ago, Kaylee discovered that Wes's father recently died, leaving Wes's older brother Levi in charge of the luxury resort. Wes ran the golf course, and two of his other brothers managed programs on the property.

Entering Wes's life after such a loss was the worst possible timing. But Kaylee's wedding was in a couple of months, and it was now or never.

She trudged forward, golf bag on her shoulder, and stopped a few feet behind him. He hadn't noticed her yet, and she took the opportunity to soak in the man she'd once loved more than anything.

Wes's casual stance, the light smile that played on the corner of his mouth as he chatted with the other golfer—this was the fun-loving guy she remembered. She couldn't see his deep blue eyes with part of his back to her, but she remembered the glint in them when he'd steal a kiss. Or the depths they could hold when he squeezed her hand while making love to her...

A warm shiver spread along her lower spine. This was a

bad idea, tracking down Wes. And taking golf lessons from him? Maybe closure wasn't so important after all. Not when unwanted sparks filled her whenever Wes was near. He evoked emotions she thought were gone, but apparently, they'd just been dormant. And they were emotions she needed to forget if she had any hope of starting a new life with Eddy.

Kaylee was about to abandon the entire idea of lessons with Wes, when his body stiffened.

He turned slowly and faced her, his gaze dropping to her lips before moving to her cheeks—where her face still burned from those stupid memories of them together.

If he'd tensed from her presence a moment ago, he hid it now. Wes didn't fidget, didn't break his stare. His demeanor was cool. Meanwhile, her temperature had risen and her legs felt wobbly.

"Is this still a good time?" Her voice came out high and nervous. She cleared her throat. "I can return later if you're busy." *Or not return at all.* Darn Eddy and his obsession with golf on their honeymoon. What was it with men and that sport?

Kaylee might have moved on, but Wes had stolen a piece of her heart. That didn't mean they were right for each other. She would never forget the pain she'd suffered during and after their relationship.

Her plan had been to finally put the past to rest...once she told Wes what she should have said years ago. But she couldn't explain things until they were on better terms. The truth was too personal and raw to mention while Wes looked at her like she was mud stuck to the bottom of his shoe. Which meant she had to tough things out, no matter how uncomfortable being around Wes would be.

"Now is fine," he said.

He sent a catch-you-later nod to the man he'd been talking to and looked over Kaylee's shoulder, his gaze settling somewhere beyond. A sweet smile spread across his face.

Kaylee's heart lurched. Wes's smiles had always melted her, and the effect they still had on her rattled Kaylee—reminding her again of why she'd fallen for Wes all those years ago. But Wes's smile hadn't been directed at her.

Kaylee turned to see a little girl—maybe four years old?—walking toward them. The child was carrying a small set of clubs, her hair pulled into a braided ponytail that swung back and forth with her determined pace. She had the same intense expression Wes used to sport when he headed out for a round of golf.

"Bella, meet Kaylee," Wes said.

The young girl gave Kaylee a once-over. "Is she training too?"

Wes frowned. "Course not. Kaylee's nowhere near your skill level. I'll be training you and giving Kaylee tips. She can watch your form as an example of how it's done."

Bella grinned.

"Show me how it's done?" Kaylee said quietly for only Wes's ears. "By a four-year-old?"

"Five," Wes said, and crossed his arms over his chest, widening his stance. "Bella's small for her age, but don't let the size fool you. She's my best student."

Kaylee caught the smirk on his lips.

Awesome. Not only was spending time with Wes going to be awkward, but he planned to make her look like an idiot. She supposed that in his mind she deserved it. Which she could handle. What she couldn't handle was going the rest of her life without clearing the air with him.

Even so, Wes training a little girl was odd. He'd never

much cared for anyone else's game, always too focused on his own. "You're really teaching kids now?"

"New program at the club. It's not so bad. Especially with students like Bella."

Bella took a practice swing. And she was really good.

"That's it," Wes called. "Keep your arm straight like I taught you last week. Slow and easy."

Bella lined up a ball, raised her club, and swung, sending the ball way the hell out onto the driving range.

Kaylee coughed into her palm, holding back a smile. "Okay, you're right. She's talented."

Wes glanced over. "Nervous?"

"Not at all." Kaylee crossed her arms below her breasts. "I've got skills too."

He cut her a look, his gaze dropping briefly to her chest, then rising slowly back to her eyes. He shook his head. "I don't think so."

Dammit. He must have seen her hitting balls at the driving range the other day.

The truth was that Kaylee royally sucked at golf. Not that she'd admit that to Wes.

He smiled proudly at another ball Bella launched into the atmosphere. "Good job," he called.

Kaylee swallowed. And swallowed again. Because, suddenly, something else occurred to her. Wes wasn't only teaching Bella for the fun of it or because he admired her talent...he genuinely cared for the little girl.

Seeing her self-centered ex teach a little girl how to play his favorite sport had an odd effect on Kaylee's chest—a pinching, pulling sensation that made her heart ache.

Bella grinned over her shoulder, seeking Wes's approval.

He nodded and said, "Practice what I taught you while I get Kaylee set up."

Kaylee squared her shoulders. She would not let Wes acting adorable with a child affect her. Lots of men liked kids. This was no different.

Except it *was* different, because this was Wes.

He'd always been self-focused. He might have said he loved her when they'd dated, but his actions had made it clear she'd never been a priority.

Kaylee pulled out her golf glove and slipped it on. "How often does Bella practice?"

Wes shrugged. "Her parents come here often. I've been instructing her off and on all summer. That girl's gonna be a pro someday."

For a moment, Kaylee just stared. He almost seemed to care more about a small child's success than his own. And that was just crazy.

"What if she decides to quit golf and take up dance?" Kaylee was goading him like she used to do. Only now she wasn't sure how he'd take it.

Wes snarled. "No way. Not if I have anything to say about it."

Kaylee laughed. He'd taken it exactly how he used to—with an air of arrogance and disgruntlement. Though deep down, he'd always been a softy at heart.

Her smile faded. Didn't matter if he'd had a good heart. Sometimes that wasn't enough.

Keeping things light, she said, "You never know, Wes. Women change their minds."

His expression fell and his mouth hardened. "I'm familiar with women changing their minds."

Shit. She'd not meant to go there so soon. She was still trying to get them back on good terms.

Kaylee turned and grabbed a golf club. "So what should I work on first? My swing? My stance?"

Wes looked off into the distance, as though he knew she was changing the subject. When he peered back, his gaze was neutral. "Your posture, form, and just about everything suck, so we'll start at the beginning. Right where I started Bella." He grinned smugly.

"You enjoy rubbing in how bad I am?"

"Do you really want the answer to that?"

"No," she grumbled, and set a ball on a wooden tee she'd shoved into the soil.

"Hold up." Wes walked over and grabbed her club. "First of all, use your pitching wedge, not the driver. You need to build up to the longer clubs."

He dropped the driver into her golf bag, grabbed a shorter, smaller club, and handed it to her. Wes bent over and plucked the wooden tee she'd used to prop up the ball. He set the ball flush with the grass instead. Which, in Kaylee's limited experience, was harder to hit from.

Wes scanned her body.

And her chest warmed, belly dropping.

The first time Kaylee had met Wes, he'd zeroed in on her at a college party and asked her to dance. That dance had turned into a kiss, which had turned into an overnight stay at her house that lasted all weekend. They were inseparable for two years. And it seemed her body remembered the effect he had on her and responded accordingly.

Be strong. You're engaged! Wes was observing her golf stance, not checking her out—though she was pretty sure he'd given her a boob check earlier. Didn't matter.

"Let me see your grip," he said.

She held out her club and showed him the grip her fiancé had taught her.

Wes shifted her hand slightly, his warm palm grazing the skin on her bared fingers. A spark of heat swept up Kaylee's arm. Wes's eyes shot to hers, as though he felt it too.

He let go of her hand and cleared his throat. "Not bad. Give me your starting position."

Kaylee went through the motions of her setup and swung the club the way she'd practiced.

Wes pressed his fingers to his forehead and shook his head. "Jesus, Kaylee. Are you sure you want to take up golf?"

She dropped her club to the turf. "Yes. Now are you going to show me or not?"

"Is this all because your *fiancé* wants you to play?"

She noted the emphasis on her intended. Her engagement had gone over about as well as she'd expected—not well at all. Wes had always dominated the room when they'd been together. There had never been space for other guys, even if she wanted to date someone else. "I've always wanted to learn, but you weren't..."

His brow furrowed. "I wasn't what?"

She huffed out a sigh. "You were always too busy in college to teach me. I could have gone to someone else, but I wanted to learn from you."

He stared at her for a long moment, ocean-blue eyes unreadable. "Keep your arms down, feet shoulder width apart, and bend your knees."

She blinked, then did as he said. Because, despite their rocky past, he was trying.

The rest of the lesson went a lot like that. Wes barked orders at Kaylee and cooed over Bella's—admittedly incredible—form. Bella kicked ass, and by the end of the lesson, Kaylee wanted to be Bella when she grew up. Because at present, Kaylee still missed the ball more often than she made contact.

"Your form is better," Wes mumbled. "Can't hit for shit, but form is important. The rest will come."

It was a backward compliment, but she'd take it because Wes didn't dole them out often. Kaylee grinned.

Wes's eyes widened, and he glanced away. "It'll take practice." He grabbed her club and slipped it into her golf bag. "*Lots* of practice, if you plan to be out on the course in... When did you say you're getting married?" She heard the edge in his tone.

Kaylee rattled off her wedding date, mere months away, which suddenly seemed to loom over her. There was so much to get done, not the least of which was getting close enough to her ex to make things right. And now Eddy was putting pressure on her to keep up with him on the golf course, which seemed about as insurmountable as warming Wes up.

Wes stared without responding, like he was silently attempting to drill some message into her head with his eyes. That he hated her? That he wanted her gone? What?

Some things about Wes were the same. In other ways, he was an entirely different man. More hardened. Less trusting.

"If you want to be ready by then," he finally said, "you had better practice in between lessons."

"I can come every day if needed."

Wes flinched. After a moment, he said, "I've gotta get back to Bella," and turned and walked away.

Kaylee's shoulders sank. Things were awkward, when at one point they'd been the opposite. Kaylee had never felt a connection like the one she'd had with Wes. Until the end, when everything in her life had crumpled.

It had taken a long time to recover from the loss. She planned to make things right between her and Wes.

It was the only way to move on with a clear conscience.

CHAPTER TWO

Sweat dripped down Kaylee's forehead and temples. Her golf shirt stuck to her breasts and back, and she was panting lightly. From hitting golf balls. Who would have thought?

"Bent arm... Nope, butt's out too far." Bella giggled. "Kaylee, I just showed you how high to hold the club." Bella sat on her princess perch at the far end of the driving range, barking orders. Wes's idea for when Kaylee practiced between lessons.

Kaylee dropped the head of her club to the grass and looked over. "Bella, anyone ever tell you you're a slave driver?"

Bella laughed, her giggles making her body shake on the low storage unit where she sat.

Kaylee sighed with a smile. "I'm happy I amuse you." She set up another shot. "Not like my arms are about to fall off," she said dramatically. "And my butt hurts. Why does my butt hurt?"

More giggles from the peanut gallery.

"You're not used to using your ass muscles?"

Wes.

Kaylee swung around to find Wes standing behind her, watching the show. "What are you doing here?"

He crossed his arms. "I work here. Oh, and I own the resort. But to be more specific, I'm here to grab my star pupil." He looked at Bella. "Good work. Kaylee's form is marginally better. Keep it up and you'll be my next assistant pro."

Bella hopped off the three-foot wooden structure and went to Wes's side. She tugged on his shirt, and he leaned down.

He nodded at something Bella whispered into his ear. "Set up your clubs first," he told her.

Wes watched Bella run off then turned to Kaylee. "If you're that sore, you might want to call it a day. You look a little flushed." He smirked.

Kaylee wiped her brow. "Gee, thanks."

Still grinning, Wes walked after Bella.

Kaylee was happy things had softened between them these last couple of days. Wes didn't appear as angry as he'd been when she first arrived at Club Tahoe. But that didn't mean things were comfortable enough for a deep talk. At this point, it was hard to imagine they would ever be, but Kaylee had hope.

She collected her golf clubs and lifted the heavy bag onto her shoulder. Under the weight of her clubs and with a sore ass, Kaylee lumbered toward the pro shop. Who knew golf was such a physical sport? It appeared so easy when Wes played in college or when she watched tournaments on TV with Eddy.

Just past the shop, Kaylee stopped to use the restroom and found Wes standing beside the women's locker room.

His arms were crossed and his head was bent, as though he were waiting.

"You okay there?" she asked, and craned her neck to the side. "Men's restroom seems open. You sure you wouldn't rather use that one?"

His mouth twisted. "Funny. I'm waiting for Bella."

Kaylee's smile fell. "Is she okay?"

Wes lifted his back off the wall, arms still crossed. "She's fine. She, uh...likes me to walk her to the restroom. Doesn't want to be alone. Thinks the bathrooms are creepy."

Kaylee's lips parted, but no words came out. Wes, her tall, cocky, athletic ex-boyfriend, was waiting outside the women's bathroom...so that a little girl wouldn't be afraid? "Who are you?" she finally said.

Before he could react, Bella emerged.

"Hi, Kaylee," she said happily, and tugged on Wes's shirt. "Come on, Wes. Let's go crush it."

Wes started to follow Bella to the driving range, but Kaylee touched his arm, stopping him—and a shock of attraction ran up her body.

That was getting annoying.

Wes looked down at her hand, and she quickly dropped it.

She glanced after Bella. "That little girl has you wrapped around her finger," she said with a smile.

He shrugged. "She needs me. And she's a good kid. You got a problem with that?"

Kaylee swallowed, her smile dropping. She shook her head. "No—I'm just surprised."

"Well, don't be. You don't know me anymore." He stormed off, and Kaylee stood there, eyes growing misty.

He was still so angry, and it hurt, but it was also going to make what she'd come here to do more difficult. Even so, watching Bella and Wes together was the sweetest thing she'd seen in a long time—and it broke her heart. Because when Kaylee saw Wes treat Bella with such gentleness, she worried she'd been wrong about him all those years ago.

———

KAYLEE ENTERED HER PARENTS' Tahoe house after wiping sweat—and a few tears—from her face in the golf course restroom. She'd never have expected Wes to be so caring with a child. And it messed with her head.

"Hello?" she called out.

"Up here," Eddy said from the second floor.

Her parents' house was a two-story split-level with a large fireplace, open floor plan, and ceiling-high corner windows with a view of the forest. She loved this place. It felt more like home than the one she'd grown up in. Yet she'd avoided it for years.

At the top of the landing, Kaylee caught sight of Eddy in the spare catchall room, lifting weights without a shirt on.

"How was the driving range?" He forced out a breath and inhaled slowly for his next repetition of arm curls.

Enlightening, she wanted to say, but that might open up a can of worms she wasn't ready to talk about. "Hot. Sweaty. Kind of painful. I'm still sore from my lessons the other day."

Eddy set down the weights he'd been using. "No pain, no gain." He huffed out a chuckle. "And you need the work."

She pouted. "Don't rub it in. I'm getting enough grief from Wes and Bella."

"Bella?"

"Another student at the range." No way in hell Kaylee

would admit she was getting schooled by a five-year-old. "What do you want to do tonight?"

Eddy walked over and leaned down, kissing her on the neck. He smacked his lips, and his face pinched. "Salty. What do you say you hop in the shower and then I rock your world?"

Eddy was "salty" too, but she didn't mention it. Wouldn't have mattered, because she wasn't in the mood for sex. Not while she was having inappropriate physical responses to her ex. But that was just it: those responses were autonomic—the whole pheromone thing. Nothing she could control. And she knew better when it came to Wes. They weren't a good fit.

Everything would be fine once she and Eddy married and left Lake Tahoe. For now, she would deal with the awkwardness. "I'd rather we hang and watch TV."

"Babe, I told you. I'm going out with the guys tomorrow night. They're only in town for a couple of days, and I leave the following morning at the butt crack of dawn for my trip. If I don't tap that tonight, it'll be weeks before you get laid."

She rolled her eyes. "Have we been together so long that you don't even try to woo me anymore?"

He parted his lips in a silent *what?*

"Besides, I can handle a few weeks of no sex. Can you?"

He huffed out a breath. "Of course." He swatted her on the ass and headed toward the master bedroom. "That's what my right hand is for."

Kaylee sank onto the mattress and took off her shoes, because, despite not being in the mood, she *was* taking a shower. "This will be good for us," she called. "It'll make the wedding night that much more special." And maybe make Eddy more appreciative.

Eddy had gotten lazy over the last year when it came to

making her feel important. It was probably normal for couples to stop trying as hard after a while, but Kaylee wasn't even married to Eddy yet. And she had a hang-up about not feeling important enough to her significant other.

"*What?*" he yelled. "No way in hell I'm waiting that long to get laid."

She supposed asking Eddy to wait two months until their wedding was a bit much. But she didn't want her current relationship to end up like her last. She wanted to be appreciated. Which was all the more reason to resolve lingering issues with Wes so she could focus on a future with Eddy.

CHAPTER THREE

The next night, Wes pulled down the bill of his baseball cap and walked across the Fireside Lounge to where his four brothers sat in the corner, wearing baseball hats too.

He sank into one of the cushioned lounge chairs that looked as if it had been built with rugged logs, but was actually made of lightweight faux-wood material to go with the elegant log-cabin appeal of the club. "Whose idea was it to wear the hats? We're more conspicuous in these things."

"Bran's," Levi said.

Levi was Wes's oldest brother and the CEO of Club Tahoe, now that their father had passed. And man did Levi have a rocky start filling those shoes after being a firefighter for years. But Levi's assistant turned girlfriend, Emily, had made the transition easier.

Emily Wright kicked ass. She was a thin blonde, but that girl was no pushover. "Where's the velvet hammer?" Wes asked.

Levi tried to hide his smile. "Stop calling my girlfriend that."

"What?" Wes said. "She's a ballbreaker."

Levi chuckled. "Maybe you should try being nicer."

Wes leaned back and pointed a thumb at his chest. "I'm a perfect gentleman."

"Except when you're trying to get laid," Bran said from his corner of the table. He sipped a beer, the bill of his cap pulled low.

Wes might have slept with a few women these last couple of years. Okay, he'd gotten laid as often as he could. Nothing numbed the mind better than a hot and dirty orgasm. "These stupid hats were your idea?"

Bran was the pretty one. Technically, none of the brothers needed help getting women, but women threw themselves at Bran. Which was seriously fucked up, considering he couldn't read the finer sex to save his life. Bran had no clue when a woman was coming on to him.

Bran frowned. "The hats were supposed to keep the attention away. It's been like a damned manhunt in this place since Adam's engagement party." He sank lower in his chair, which wasn't easy. Wes and his brothers were all over six feet.

Adam, Wes's second oldest brother, had recently held his elaborate engagement party at the club. But it went down during a rocky period for Levi. He'd still been coming to terms with his feelings for Emily. So when Hunt, their youngest brother, kissed Emily at the party to get a rise out of Levi, Levi had flipped the fuck out, starting a fistfight right in the middle of the festivities.

Adam pushed up the bill of his cap and shot Levi an annoyed look. He wore a suit and must have come straight from work at Blue Casino, one of their competitors in town. "Speaking of my engagement party, just because Hayden forgave you, that doesn't mean I have. You owe me for that stupid fight, Levi. I'll settle for free food at the wedding this spring."

Levi shook his head. "For four hundred guests? That's a bit rich, don't you think?"

Adam shrugged. "You can afford it."

Levi grunted. "Hunt should have kept his damned lips off my girlfriend."

Hunt raised his palms, his baseball cap turned backward. He wore a Club Tahoe T-shirt with jeans and was the most casual of the group, having come from the dock and beach area he managed at the resort. "She wasn't your girlfriend at the time. And I've apologized."

Needless to say, Adam was still pissed at both Levi and Hunt, and the gossip from that night had gotten out of hand. Levi had worried their bungle would take away business, but it had only grown—at least among the female population.

Local women were well aware of the five wealthy brothers who owned and ran Club Tahoe Resort. Good thing, too, because it made hooking up a hell of a lot easier. Wes barely had to put the moves on a woman before she was dragging him into her bed.

Since the engagement party, though, there were actual groupies hanging out in the lounge to get a glimpse of him and his brothers. Or get laid. Wes was all for it, but some of his brothers were less enthusiastic—Levi and Adam, who weren't single. And Bran, the dumbass, was uncomfortable with the whole thing for some unknown reason.

It would be a perfectly acceptable response if Bran were gay. But no, he was just awkward around aggressive women. Meanwhile, Wes loved the attention. Aggressive women made going from point A—the talking stage—to point B—the getting-laid stage—so much easier.

Occasionally, Wes and his brothers agreed to avoid the lounge and drink beers off-site, but that wasn't always practical. The stupid hats were Bran's failed attempt to keep a low profile.

Nearby, one of the groupies crossed and uncrossed her legs, glancing provocatively in Wes's direction. "Nice try, but the hats aren't working." His gaze snagged on a beautiful brunette entering the lounge in a black dress that clung to her curves, and his smug grin fell. "What the hell is she doing here?"

Levi looked over. "Isn't that your ex-girlfriend? Kaylee, right?"

Wes stared at the table and picked up his beer. He took a deep swig. But his gaze slipped back to Kaylee, who lingered near the entrance.

This wasn't normal. Him giving Kaylee lessons. Her planning her wedding at the club.

Hunt leaned on his forearms, angling his head to the side. "Pretty. Is she single?"

Wes shot him a death glare.

Hunt chuckled. "Just checking."

"She's *engaged*. Otherwise, I wouldn't care what you did."

Hunt coughed into his hand and muttered, "Bullshit."

Wes might have some fucked-up feelings when it came to Kaylee, but he didn't *want* her. What he wanted was to know why she was here.

Enough of this bullshit. It was time he found out. Wes stood, and Adam jumped up too.

"Whoa, there," Adam said. "We can't afford another fight at the club."

Wes rolled his eyes. "Simmer down. I'm giving Kaylee golf lessons. I just need to check in with her."

"Then why do you look ready to rip off someone's head?"

"I always look this way," Wes said, and walked toward Kaylee, who was peering around as though she were searching for someone.

Right as Wes neared, McDouche walked up behind her and put his arm around her waist.

Kaylee visibly stiffened. "I'm only here to say goodbye to Eddy."

Her fiancé looked down at her questioningly—probably because Wes was radiating all kinds of kill vibes. "Everything okay?"

"Of course," Wes said. "Lessons are going well, with Bella's assistance."

Kaylee gave Wes a halfhearted frown.

She couldn't be happy that he had a five-year-old teaching her how to swing her golf club. But if she wanted his help, she'd have to deal with his tactics. Besides, Bella could kick Kaylee's ass on the course, so it wasn't a bad pairing.

"There's that Bella person again," McDouche said. "Who is she?"

"No one," Kaylee said at the same time Wes said, "My protégée."

Her fiancé nodded. "Great. She must be good, then."

Kaylee pulled away from McDouche and touched Wes's elbow. "Why don't we talk in the lobby? Eddy's spending time with his friends tonight. I should get going anyway."

"Good idea, babe." Eddy leaned over and kissed Kaylee on the cheek.

Wes's breathing increased and his heart pounded hard

in his chest. He walked away before he did something stupid, like attack Kaylee's fiancé for no good reason.

Wes waited for Kaylee outside the lounge in one of the seating areas of the large Club Tahoe lobby. He spread his arms across the back of a velvet couch and crossed his ankle over his knee. Relaxed, that was what he was. His ex didn't rile him up. He was a man in control.

Kaylee entered the lobby and surveyed the space until her gaze landed on him. She walked over, and Wes couldn't help admiring her.

Still fucking beautiful. Still stole his breath.

But he shut that shit down. Didn't want or need it.

Kaylee sat across from him on the edge of the opposite couch, her legs pressed together and slanted to the side. "What did you want to talk about?"

Like she didn't know. "Why are you really here?"

Her face flushed. "I— You know why I'm here. I'm getting married at the resort, and Eddy wants me to take golf lessons. With Bella's tutelage, I might actually hit the ball on our honeymoon." Her mouth curved into an ironic smile, but it was a shaky one.

If Wes didn't know better, he'd think she was holding something back. "Does it bother you that I'm having Bella give you pointers?"

"Bella's adorable and very encouraging. *However,* I understand why you paired me with her." She gave him a pointed look.

"Because she could teach you a thing or two?"

"Because you want to humiliate me... And I understand where the anger is coming from." She twined her fingers together, her knuckles turning white. "It's partly why I'm here."

Now they were getting somewhere. Because Kaylee

sure as shit hadn't come to Club Tahoe to get married. Her family was from a small town, but they had money. She could have gotten married at any fancy resort. She didn't need the club. "Continue."

Kaylee swallowed. "I never liked how things ended between us. But at the time, I wasn't capable of talking to you about it. I hoped to do that now."

Wes attempted to remain cool, but his adrenaline from earlier hadn't subsided, and he wanted to tell her to cut the bullshit and spill whatever it was she'd hidden from him. He needed this. Needed to know the truth. He wanted his life back. Because Adam was right: Wes was angry.

He thought he'd moved on, but the more time he spent with Kaylee, the more he realized she'd ruined him in some fundamental way. That was the part he couldn't forgive her for. "So talk."

She huffed out a frustrated breath. "This is why I waited to say anything." Kaylee unfolded her hands and gestured to him harshly. "I won't talk to you while you're looking at me with such hostility. What I have to say is important."

He crossed his arms and dropped his foot to the floor. Seeing another man kiss Kaylee, even if it had only been on the cheek, had pissed him off. And thinking of his past with her wasn't helping either. Then again, he'd already been pissed. Had been an irritable ass for most of the last four years. "You're dragging this out. Just tell me what you came here to say, and get married somewhere else."

Kaylee jerked back. "I'm getting married at Club Tahoe because it's beautiful. Not because you own it."

"*Right.*"

She shook her head. "This was a mistake. If I try to explain things now, you won't hear me." She stood abruptly.

"Where are you going?" He wanted to jump up after her, but he stayed put, attempting to remain calm, though his head pounded with rage.

"Home." She gestured toward the lounge. "Eddy has plans with his friends. He's leaving for a long business trip at dawn. I only came to say goodbye."

Wes scrunched up his face. He was still fuming over her refusal to talk about the past, but something she said niggled him. "Your fiancé is spending his last night in town...with his friends?"

Her eyes narrowed. "Don't judge me, Wes Cade. Eddy's been there for me. Which is more than I can say for you."

There was the sass he remembered from college. Even if it was misdirected. Then again, that part of her only came out when they'd been alone. To the rest of the world, and before Wes had gotten to know her, she had been shy and sweet. It seemed Wes brought out the fire in her. Which worked when they used to be alone, but not in this situation.

Screw calm. He jumped up and leaned down until their heads were inches apart. "Is that why you left me? Jesus, Kaylee, I had the biggest tournament of my life on the horizon. I didn't have a shitload of time on my hands, but if you'd needed something, you could have just said so."

"What I needed was more than you were capable of giving."

Were those tears rimming her eyes? "You don't know that."

She swallowed. "I didn't know for sure at the time. But I worried about how you'd react. I was confused. Scared."

She'd known him pretty well back then. Still... "It's been years. Why don't you tell me what you should have said then? It shouldn't matter at this point how I react.

You're about to get married, and I've moved on a hundred times over."

She flinched.

Okay, that had been harsh.

"I— No," she said. "This is wrong. Forget it." She spun to leave.

Wes grabbed her by the arm. "Hell no."

"Everything okay over here?" Eddy approached from the direction of the lounge, looking from Kaylee to Wes's grip on her. "I came to walk you to the car."

"I was just leaving," she said, and pulled her arm free. It didn't take much, because Wes hadn't been holding her tightly.

Wes shoved his hands in his pockets and smoothed his features, nodding to Eddy. He watched them make their way to the entrance, Kaylee with a stiff back and Eddy with his slimy arm draped over her shoulders.

Her fiancé was leaving for a trip? Good. Kaylee wouldn't be able to pull another disappearing act. Wes would have plenty of time to find out why she was here without interruptions—and then she could leave.

Because there was no way Wes could prepare for the pro qualifying tournament tensed up the way he'd been since her arrival.

CHAPTER FOUR

After Kaylee walked away with her fiancé, Wes returned to his brothers' table, jerked out a chair, and slumped into it.

"How was the chat with your ex?" Levi said sarcastically.

Jackass. Levi's new girlfriend was Levi's ex's little sister. And boy had that been a hot topic. Levi probably found Wes's situation amusing, with Wes in the hot seat now.

"Fine." Wes flagged the waitress. He needed another beer. Make that a shot and a beer.

"So, what's the deal?"

"No deal. Just trying to figure out why she showed up at my resort."

Hunt flipped a bottle cap on the table, then flipped it again. "*Our* resort. And this wouldn't be the girl you dated in college, would it?"

Wes cut him a look. "How do you even know that?"

Hunt shrugged. "She was your last serious girlfriend. And she was hot. Kind of hard to forget. Though she chopped off her hair." Hunt scanned beyond Wes, as though searching her out.

"She's still hot," Wes said, not helping to dissuade his idiot brothers from asking more questions.

"You gonna try and hit that?" Hunt asked.

"Hell no. And don't talk about her that way." Wes ordered from the waitress and returned his attention to Hunt. "Kaylee and I have unfinished business, is all. She's going to explain some shit and be on her way. She's messing with my golf chi."

Bran groaned and peeled the label off his beer. "Quit blaming that poor girl for why your game is in the can. It's not her fault."

"The fuck it isn't." The waitress set a shot in front of Wes, and he threw it back.

Emily, Levi's girlfriend, snuck up behind Levi and pressed her finger to her lips. She covered Levi's eyes with her hands.

Levi grinned and reached around, grabbing the backs of Emily's legs, encased in a dark, slim skirt. She was a bit of a workaholic and likely just getting off.

"Emily..." Levi drew out her name in a low tone.

She laughed and dropped her hands. "How did you know it was me?"

Levi hooked his arm around her waist and pulled her onto his lap. "I smelled you." He waggled his eyebrows.

Wes snarled. *Really? This? Now?*

He shot a look at Hunt, who rolled his eyes too.

Adam, meanwhile, stared unerringly at Wes. "What if Kaylee still loves you?"

Wes choked on a gulp of beer. "What?"

Adam sat back in his chair and crossed his arms over his

chest, his dress shirt rolled just below his elbows. "It's possible. Maybe that's why she's here."

"With her fiancé in tow? I don't think so. And if you're right, who cares? It wouldn't change anything." But that was a lie.

It would mean something.

All these years, Wes had thought Kaylee had fallen out of love with him. One moment they were talking about the future, and the next his ass was hitting the pavement after being dumped. If she still cared about him, it wouldn't change things exactly...but it might ease some of his anger over the past.

"Who's Kaylee?" Emily asked, then stole a sip of Levi's beer.

"Wes's ex-girlfriend," Levi said.

Emily's forehead scrunched. "Wes had a girlfriend?"

"Yes, I had a girlfriend," Wes said. "Is that so hard to believe?"

"Well...yeah," she said. "I've seen you go home with dozens of women since I started working here. I can't picture you as a one-woman guy. Did you cheat on her?"

Wes set his beer on the table with a thunk. "No, I didn't cheat on her. What is this? Bash Wes Night? Can we drop it, please?"

Adam looked to Bran, who looked to Levi.

"Nope," Hunt said, grinning. "This shit is good entertainment." He nodded at a beautiful groupie staring their way. "That woman's been eyeing you since you returned from your little chat with Kaylee. Why don't you go over there?"

"Not in the mood."

Hunt smacked his hand on the table. "I knew it!" He

raised his arms triumphantly. "Wes wants his ex. Who wants to place bets?"

Bran shook his head. "Leave him alone."

"Just because I don't feel like a woman's company tonight," Wes said, "that doesn't mean I want my ex back."

"Really?" Hunt looked past him. "Then you don't mind that her fiancé is about to hook up with that blonde over there?"

The fuck? Wes whipped his head around.

Sure enough, McDouche was hanging out with his friends and had his hand on a woman's ass. He whispered something in the woman's ear then looked around.

To see who was watching?

Wes would bet anything that Kaylee hadn't informed her fiancé about the extent of her and Wes's past. Ex-boyfriends were competition, and Eddy would be more circumspect with this chick in the lounge if he knew Wes had been an intimate part of Kaylee's past. Instead, the guy was openly hitting on the woman, no cares at all, now that his fiancée had gone home.

But Eddy wasn't stupid. Before Kaylee had left, he'd made sure to touch her in Wes's presence and mark his territory. And to make sure her new golf instructor wasn't looking while he hit on another woman, because the guy was darting his gaze every few seconds while he whispered in the woman's ear.

Maybe the baseball hats were more effective than Wes thought? Because Eddy missed Wes staring at him from the corner of the room.

Wes and his brothers were in the back, somewhat hidden, thanks to Bran's insistence on keeping a low profile, but Wes stared down at the table anyway when Eddy peered in their direction. When Wes looked up, Eddy was slipping out the side door, and he wasn't alone.

"Son of a bitch." Wes's jaw clenched. "That fucker."

"Bets, anyone?" Hunt said. "Fifty bucks says Wes and Kaylee are back together by the end of the week."

Wes ignored his brothers, even though a couple of them were actually placing bets. Dumbasses.

He waited and glanced at the door every few seconds for Kaylee's fiancé to return. The hum of chatter in the lounge was just that—a steady stream of white noise. Wes couldn't focus on any conversation. Not while this shit with Kaylee's fiancé was going down.

It took McDouche twenty-two minutes to walk back inside, and when he did, part of his button-down shirt was untucked and he wiped lipstick off his mouth. The woman he'd been with walked in behind him, her hair ruffled. She said something to the others and headed toward the women's restroom.

One of Eddy's cronies pointed at his fly. Eddy laughed, turned around, and slyly pulled up his zipper.

"Motherfucker."

"Yeah," Hunt said, eyeing Wes. "That's what I thought."

Wes gripped his beer bottle. "Not my problem."

Emily was sitting in her own seat now, sipping a gin and tonic, but Levi had pulled her chair close, his leg parked behind it. "Wait." She stared at McDouche. "I know that guy. He and his fiancée came to see me about their wedding. *She's* your ex-girlfriend?"

Wes shrugged noncommittally.

Emily curled her dainty lip and leaned forward. "I think that woman gave him a blowjob. There are lipstick marks on his pants."

Hunt chuckled. "That's a foregone conclusion."

"That is so messed up." Emily stared at Wes. "You have to say something to your ex-girlfriend."

Wes sighed. He wanted to punch Eddy in the fucking face. But to tell Kaylee?

No. Not a good idea.

Things were better between them. At least while they were on the course with Bella. But their conversation earlier proved tension still existed.

Okay, mostly on Wes's part. He was pissed. And she knew it. If Wes said something about her fiancé, she might not believe him.

Still, this was fucked up.

Maybe Emily was right. And Bran too. The past was the past. Kaylee wanted to talk, but he'd been an ass to her, and now she didn't feel comfortable opening up.

He dug his fingers into his hair. She'd been a great girlfriend...until the end. And he'd loved her.

He still couldn't see himself telling her that her fiancé had cheated, but he could try to be more civil.

She deserved that much.

CHAPTER FIVE

Wes headed for the driving range at the time he'd agreed to meet Kaylee, and found her already there with Bella. His star pupil was showing Kaylee how to reposition her backswing.

Bella shook her head. "Not like that, Kaylee. Watch." Bella demonstrated the move with her small club perfectly.

Kaylee raised an eight iron, attempting to mimic Bella, but her angle was off.

Bella set her club to the side and jumped up, trying to push Kaylee's club higher and to the left, but she was too short.

"I got it," Wes said.

Kaylee whipped around and looked at him warily. "Wasn't sure if you'd show today."

He touched her elbow, and she flinched, her green eyes widening.

Wes swallowed, ignoring the familiar, clean scent of her —and the heat that licked his body when she was near. He raised the club to the proper position. "Like this," he said, and stepped back. "Try again."

She did as he said, and her position this time wasn't half bad.

He nodded. "Good. Now bring it back exactly like that ten times. Then take a full practice swing."

Kaylee practiced her backswing, and Wes turned to Bella. He sank onto his haunches, putting him eye level with her. "What's going on? You're not due here until later."

Bella crossed her small arms and pouted. "My parents are at the casino. They told me to go play. I don't want to play. I want to hang out with you." She appeared anxious.

Wes glanced at Kaylee, who'd paused in her practice and was staring at them. He focused on Bella. "You can hang with me. We'll give Kaylee some tips, okay? At some point, though, make sure to check in with your parents and tell them where you are."

Bella nodded enthusiastically and ran to grab her clubs at the end of the driving range.

Kaylee practiced her full swing, and it was much better than when he'd first seen her with a club. "That was really sweet," she said without looking over.

Wes turned to make sure Bella wasn't near. "Her parents are assholes. Bella's a good kid."

Kaylee nodded, but her shoulders had stiffened, and it was affecting the way she held the club.

And here was his opportunity to be civil. "Everything okay?"

"Fine." She took another practice swing. "I'm just glad Bella has you. She'll remember it, you know? It'll make a difference that you were there for her."

He wasn't used to being there for anyone aside from his brothers. And, at one time, Kaylee. Only she said he'd failed her, so maybe he was wrong about that.

He crossed his arms and spread his legs, focusing on her swing. "You're lifting your front foot and bending your elbow too much."

He pointed to her elbow and showed her with his own arm how he wanted her to hold the club. "Focus on those three things: the height and position of your backswing, keeping your foot down, and making sure your elbow is straight. I'll be back in a minute."

He went to check on Bella, but his mind raced in every direction, panic settling like a blow to his chest. This was the kind of shit that had drawn Wes to Kaylee in the first place. Not many people would have given more than a second thought to Bella's situation. It didn't appear she was abused by her parents, but the little girl was lonely. And Kaylee saw it and worried for Bella.

Wes related to Bella more than he liked because of his upbringing, with a dead mother and an absent father. The friendship Kaylee had formed with Bella, the way she worried over the little girl... Wes didn't want to remember how kind Kaylee was—and all the other reasons he'd fallen for her.

He'd been raised in a mansion and left to roam a luxury resort. Lonely or not, Wes was used to getting what he wanted. And that confidence spilled over to women as well. Yet in college, whenever his ego had gotten out of hand, Kaylee would either call him out or laugh at him.

Laugh at him.

That had been enough to put his ego in check. And to have him chasing her until she was his.

Wes's physical response to Kaylee had been pretty fucking intense. Kaylee's beauty, combined with her kind heart and sass, meant he'd fallen for her hard. Until she'd let him go.

If Wes didn't know Kaylee—if she was simply some woman who'd come in for golf lessons, with her beauty and kindness—he'd have brought out his A-game and pursued her.

But Kaylee was his ex. She was engaged. And more importantly, she'd broken his heart, though he'd never admit it to her.

Wes didn't trust Kaylee. And what they'd shared had been destroyed long ago. There was no *them,* and whatever his chest was feeling had better settle the fuck down. Because he wouldn't take a second chance on her.

———

WES WATCHED Kaylee practice alongside Bella for two straight hours. Kaylee had wisps of dark hair stuck to her sweaty face and her arms were limp at her sides, while Bella seemed ready to take on another two hours of hitting balls.

Kaylee held up her arm and stared at him. "My hands are locked in a claw position. I think I need to stop for the day or I might lose the use of my hands."

Bella swung her driver in the next lane over, clocking her ball way the hell out there.

"Nice one, Bella," he said.

"On second thought..." Kaylee stared at Bella wearily. "I should put away my clubs and prepare to sit in the stands. Because, really, this feels pointless next to Bella's ability."

Bella grinned from ear to ear. "Let's get lunch from the restaurant. You can come, right?"

Kaylee glanced hesitantly at Wes.

He took a deep breath. He was turning over a new leaf and letting bygones be bygones. "Join us. The course restaurant has good brats."

Kaylee laughed. "Nothing like a big sausage after a long day."

He smirked, and Kaylee blushed. She made it too damn hard to pass up grinning when she gave him innuendo ammunition like that.

"Don't even go there, Wes," Kaylee said. "I know where your head is."

He picked up Bella's small clubs. "Not me talking about large sausages."

Kaylee glanced nervously at Bella. "He's referring to the brats and beer we used to grab from a pub on campus in college. Ignore him."

"Come *oooon*," Bella said, and grabbed Kaylee's hand, dragging her toward the restaurant. "I'm staaaarved."

Kaylee looked back at her golf bag.

Wes already had Bella's on his shoulder—might as well grab Kaylee's too. "I've got it," he said.

She gave him a light smile and faced forward, walking hand in hand with Bella.

Wes's chest tightened. Again.

Fuck. Being friendly with Kaylee didn't feel safe. It felt dangerous. Blaming her for all that had gone wrong between them, and for his failed golf career, was much easier.

But probably not healthy.

He sighed. He'd always respected Kaylee. He supposed if there was any woman he could be friends with, it was her.

Wes grabbed Kaylee's golf bag and tossed it on his shoulder, following the girls to the restaurant.

CHAPTER SIX

Kaylee had spent dozens of hours with Wes practicing her golf game these last two and a half weeks. And with Bella. She loved seeing Wes with Bella; they were adorable together. But it also made her heart constrict.

Wes had said Bella's parents didn't spend much time with her, and the evidence pointed to it. Bella had been with her and Wes during every practice.

Kaylee walked from the parking lot toward the golf course, her clubs on her shoulder, and searched for Bella where she always seemed to be—at the driving range. She caught sight of the little girl's dark ponytail and small stature among the predominately male golfers, and grinned —until she saw Wes standing behind her.

With his arms crossed over his chest, muscular legs shoulder width apart, he nodded now and then at something Bella did. His mouth moved as though he were giving her pointers, and then he turned slowly, glancing around until his gaze landed on Kaylee.

A shiver swept down Kaylee's spine, and her belly

clenched. It was extremely annoying that Wes still made her heart race. She thought it would have gone away by now.

Eddy returned in a couple of days. No matter her physical response to Wes, she had an emotional tie to Eddy. He could relate to what she'd gone through, and he would be there for her in the long run.

Wes had changed—even Kaylee could see that. He'd always been a good man, but he was a better man now. More mature. More thoughtful. Especially with Bella. But Kaylee would never trust him with her heart.

"Hey there," she said, and set her clubs nearby, mentally preparing for another round of kick-Kaylee's-ass at the driving range. "What's on the docket for today?"

Wes waved another pro over. "Help Bella out for an hour?" he said to the guy.

The club pro squatted beside Bella, a smile on his face as he gestured to Bella's arm position.

Wes seemed satisfied, and grabbed Kaylee's elbow, urging her forward.

Hello, shivers. His scent—so familiar, so good—wafted to her nose, and her heart tapped around in her chest.

Just physical. Not lasting.

"We need to talk," he said.

"About golf?" She looked back at the driving range growing farther away.

"No."

They walked for a long while to a remote part of the resort beach. A jetty provided privacy, and at this point, Kaylee suspected something was up.

Wes never wanted to be alone with her. At least, that was what she'd assumed, since Bella was always there during Kaylee's lessons. Either Bella practiced all day every day because of her absentee parents, which would be disconcerting, or Wes planned for Bella to be a buffer between them.

Wes climbed onto the rocks of the jetty and reached back for her hand. He helped her up and let go as soon as she was steady. He made his way to the edge of the water.

"Is everything okay?" she asked.

Obviously it wasn't, but he was making her nervous and she wanted to get him talking. Wes was a "lay it all out there and knock a girl off her feet" kind of man. But not now. Now there were walls built, and banked anger simmered beneath the surface.

He stared at the lake for a moment, then turned to her. "It's been a couple of weeks. We've gotten along well enough, haven't we?"

They'd joked and, dare she say it, had fun on the driving range. Things hadn't been as easygoing as they used to be between them, but she'd felt the spark of a connection to Wes that she hadn't in a long while. "Yes, of course."

"Good." He nodded and let out a breath. "I'd like to know what happened when you left college. When you left me." The hard edge no longer tainted his tone, but tension filled the air.

They were alone, and she'd come to town for this very conversation. She couldn't drag it out forever, even if it was difficult to talk about.

Her hands began to shake and her body grew cold. She sank onto one of the rocks, but Wes didn't follow. He leaned against a larger stone and watched her. "Before we broke up, it was a really difficult time for me."

He shook his head, squinting. "What was hard? School? Your friends? Did something happen with your family?"

Kaylee looked out at the water, her stomach twisting.

"No. None of those things. I was going through something... physical. And I didn't know how to talk to you about it. I was afraid. You were preparing for the tour. You ate, slept, and breathed golf. It's all you talked about. Half the time, I wasn't sure you were listening to me. And then when I... When I needed you, I didn't feel safe telling you what was wrong. I worried you'd flip out."

Wes ran stiff fingers through his dark hair, the tips falling forward and touching his strong cheekbones. "Jesus, Kaylee. If something was wrong, you should have said so. Instead, you fucking *left* me."

She pulled her knees to her chest. "I couldn't trust you to take it well. I worried you'd make things worse, and I was already barely holding myself together."

"So this was about trust?" His jaw clenched and he stared back at the water, his tone as hard as the granite they sat on. "Trustworthiness doesn't seem high on your list of dating criteria."

She looked up, her eyebrows knitting together. "What are you talking about?"

"Eddy." He flung his arm carelessly. "Your fiancé."

"What does Eddy have to do with our past?"

He pinned her with a stare. "You didn't trust me, and I was devoted to you—*loved* you. And you're engaged to that...that piece of shit."

Kaylee stood. "Keep Eddy out of this! You were an absent boyfriend. That's why I didn't feel I could go to you."

"I don't see your fiancé." Wes looked around dramatically. "Where is he, Kaylee?"

"You know he's away on business." She shook her head, the air leaving her chest on a wave of disappointment. "God, Wes, I thought we were past this. But all you care about is how I hurt you. Nothing I say will change anything." She rose and spun to leave, a burning sensation prickling the back of her eyes. She couldn't talk to him—not now. Maybe not ever.

"He's cheating on you," Wes said, the malice in his tone suddenly gone.

Kaylee turned slowly back, certain she'd heard him wrong. "What?"

Wes's blue eyes churned like an ocean in a storm. "Your fiancé. He cheated on you. At least once, that I know of."

Kaylee wrapped her arms around her waist. "Are you out of your mind? You don't know Eddy."

Wes chuckled humorlessly. "I know him well enough. I know his type. I'm him half of the time." His gaze bored into hers. "Only I never cheat."

She shook her head. "You're wrong. You want Eddy to be the bad guy so it'll make you look better."

"I told my brothers you wouldn't believe me. Just like you said, you never trusted me. And what's a relationship without trust, Kaylee?"

Her lips parted, but she couldn't say anything. Because he was right. She'd not trusted him when she needed him the most. And she certainly didn't trust him now.

"Wes, I'm sorry I hurt you in college. I was in pain and not thinking straight. I had a boyfriend who didn't put me first, and it scared the hell out of me to go to you with my problem."

"So that's it? You didn't feel I spent enough time with you?"

He wasn't even listening now. "That was part of it."

The conversation had gone in the wrong direction. Why did she think he'd listen to her now, when he'd never listened before?

In some ways, Wes had changed. He was more responsible, seemed to truly care for Bella, when he had no reason to care beyond the money Bella's parents paid him for her lessons. He wasn't the same man he'd been in college. Yet in other ways, he was exactly the same. Focused to the point of missing everything.

He gave her more of that humorless laugh. "Good talk, Kaylee." Wes turned and stalked away, crossing the large boulders like he'd done it a million times. And he probably had. "Find another golf instructor. I don't want to see you again."

CHAPTER SEVEN

Kaylee slowly returned to the driving range, where her clubs sat unused. She picked them up in a daze and headed for her car. Taking golf lessons from Wes had always been a mistake.

He was right. She couldn't get married at Club Tahoe. And bringing up the past was her worst decision yet. She should have kept it where it belonged—in the past.

Only, she'd never gotten over what had happened, and she'd hoped that seeing Wes would help.

It hadn't.

She and Wes were toxic together. The hateful things he'd said about Eddy... God, what the hell was Wes thinking? Was he intentionally trying to sabotage her relationship?

Wes might have been an absent boyfriend at times, but he'd never been cruel—until today.

Except that didn't feel right either. He wasn't a cruel person. And she couldn't believe he'd try to hurt her with lies. So he must have had a reason for saying what he did. But why did he think Eddy was cheating?

Kaylee made it home on autopilot. She thought about Wes's words all evening, sleeping fitfully throughout the night. Nightmares from the past—streaks of red, the immeasurable emotional pain that had consumed every ounce of her being—were fresh and piercing. She woke gasping for air and stumbled into the bathroom, staring at her reflection until her head cleared.

The next day was no better. Kaylee wasn't trapped in nightmares from her past, but she couldn't forget Wes's accusations about Eddy. Because when she thought about it —*really* thought about it—it was possible. If Eddy had wanted to cheat on her, it wouldn't be difficult.

Eddy traveled for his job constantly, and he seemed to have friends in every state and a few countries. Kaylee assumed they were male friends. She wasn't the jealous type and had never checked. Should she have?

Eddy had come into Kaylee's life a year after she'd graduated from college. She'd met him while he was on a business trip to San Francisco. She was working for the San Francisco Women and Children's Center and living with four roommates in the city. That night, she'd gone out with her friends after work. It had been the first time she'd considered moving on and dating again.

She hadn't noticed Eddy at first. When they met, it had been nothing like meeting Wes for the first time, where his very presence smacked her silly. Eddy's charm had been slow—friendly, even. He'd asked her for her number and said he'd call the next time he was in town.

Eddy called just as he said he would, and they'd met up for dinner. When he wasn't in town, he was good about keeping in touch, texting or sending sweet notes for her birthday and other special occasions. The relationship built gradually, and before she knew it, he'd asked her to move in.

She'd been the original lease owner on her place in San Francisco, with awesome rent control. Her friends had been furious about being forced to move, but Eddy said he wanted a future with her and that they could save money if they lived at her place. It had made so much sense at the time.

Later she'd learned that Eddy *had* money. A lot of money. She wondered why he'd insisted on something that would put a wedge between her and her friends. He'd said it would help their future. Now she wasn't sure of Eddy's intent at all.

Kaylee didn't leave her parents' Tahoe house. She wore sweatpants with no makeup, biting her nails to the nub and trying to figure out what was real.

She had things in common with Eddy few people her age could relate to. She couldn't have children anymore. And Eddy couldn't either.

When their relationship progressed and he'd asked her to be his wife, she thought it must be right. Later, Eddy had also asked her to quit her job to help him socially with his business partners and clients. She'd been struggling for a sense of purpose, and his request had made her feel grateful. But she might have given up a few too many things along the way to feeling needed.

Letting go of her friends, her job—those losses were things Kaylee had been trying to wrap her head around these last six months. She'd made the sacrifices so that she and Eddy could have a happy marriage and be a family. If he'd been unfaithful to her after all she'd given up for him...

Her parents never said so, but she got the feeling Eddy wasn't their favorite person. Her old roommates had never forgiven her for letting Eddy move in at their expense. And now Wes was flat-out saying Eddy was a bad guy?

If anyone else had made the accusation, she'd have blown it off as jealousy, and she nearly did. Wes could be selfish and self-centered, but like he said, he'd been faithful. And when she thought about it, she realized he wasn't a liar. If anything, Wes could be too blunt and truthful.

"No more fucking around," Wes had said, in what felt like ages ago. "I love you and I don't want to be with anyone else. So what do you say? Be my girlfriend?" They'd only been dating a couple of weeks, and he'd been kissing her neck and squeezing her breast at the same time. Distracting her and driving her crazy. And being blunt and to the point. As usual.

The memory made Kaylee smile. When they dated, they always had their hands on each other. But his words were sincere; she'd heard it in his voice.

What Wes had said about Eddy couldn't be true. Because if it was...it would shatter the beautiful future she wanted so desperately. To be needed, cherished—and to have a family, even if it was only her and Eddy.

Kaylee rubbed her eyes, her elbows resting on the kitchen table. She should wait until Eddy returned to bring it up, but that was two days away. She couldn't ignore this that long. She'd tried, and every part of her vibrated with agitation.

Something was wrong. Wes had been furious. And not with her. *With Eddy.*

But if Kaylee asked Eddy over the phone, she wouldn't be able to watch his expression, and she needed to. Because in the back of her mind, she believed him capable of lying.

Kaylee picked up her coffee mug with shaky hands and took a sip. The warm liquid did nothing to ease the chill that had settled over her. She secured her blue fluffy robe tightly around her chest and picked up her cell phone.

After a moment's hesitation, she went to "Recents" and pressed Eddy's name.

The phone rang and Kaylee bit her thumb—all flesh with her nail chewed to the quick.

"Hey, babe!" Eddy answered.

"Hey."

"How's the wedding planning going?"

"Oh, um, it's really not. I've been practicing golf instead," she said absently, and realized it was the truth.

She'd done very little wedding planning since Eddy left, putting aside the perfect future she'd envisioned...for golf?

Eddy sighed. "Babe, I'm glad you're getting into the sport. We'll need it when we entertain my clients, but you can't forget the wedding. It's only a few weeks away, and it's got to be the shit."

Kaylee's stomach soured and she stared out at the trees. Why did their wedding have to impress people? Couldn't it just be romantic? Meaningful? Wasn't that what mattered?

Suddenly, everything he said jarred her subconscious. "What if we canceled Club Tahoe and did something small? Just a few friends and family?"

Eddy laughed. "Yeah, right. Sorry, babe, I've already invited clients. They're expecting the invitations. You sent them out, right?"

Kaylee glanced toward the front door. The invitations sat on the entry table.

She squeezed her eyes closed. "Most of the wedding is planned. I just need to finalize the details."

"Well, get on it, woman."

He was being silly, which she usually enjoyed, or at least shrugged off. But not today.

Her eyes narrowed. "Eddy, why do you want to marry me?"

He laughed. "Are you kidding?"

"Not at all."

He let out a sharp breath. "Fine, I get it. I've been gone a long time. You need reassurance, especially with the commitment we're about to make... You're beautiful, poised, and smart. Is that what you wanted to hear? Oh, and you're really hot, even when you deprive me of sex right before a long business trip." He laughed at his joke. Because he was one of those guys who laughed at his own jokes, even if they weren't funny.

Why had she never noticed what a jackass he could be?

Kaylee sensed the answer before the question left her mouth, but she asked it anyway. "Are you in love with me?"

"Jesus Christ, you're really dragging me down. Are you finished being insecure? I thought you called to check in. I've had a shitty week, but I guess I have to call someone else if I want to talk about it."

Who did he plan on calling? Another woman?

And he hadn't answered the question. He'd avoided it, drawing the conversation back to himself.

Kaylee closed her eyes. "Eddy, have you ever cheated on me?"

The phone went silent for a second. A second too long.

He chuckled again, but this one came out strained. "Of course not."

"You swear on all that's holy and your favorite pair of sweatpants?"

"Now you're just being ridiculous. Look, I'll be home in a couple of days and everything will be back to normal. I promise not to be gone so long next time. I can tell three weeks is too much."

Again, he didn't answer her question.

Her heart spasmed and her temples pounded. Talking

over the phone was no use. He wasn't giving her straight answers. She needed to ask him in person. To watch his expression, even if warning bells were blaring in her head. "See you then."

"Kaylee," he said before she ended the call, "everything's going to be okay. You've just got pre-wedding jitters."

Her head was a jumble. She mumbled something about doing laundry and ended the call.

Stupid Wes. It was as though he'd pulled a veil from her eyes—one she'd worn to survive—and suddenly everything was sharper, clearer.

And she didn't like what she saw.

CHAPTER EIGHT

Kaylee entered Club Tahoe, her stomach balled in a knot. She had an appointment with Emily Wright, a manager at the club. Emily had asked Kaylee to come in and review details for the wedding that couldn't wait any longer.

Kaylee cradled her cramping stomach and glanced around the pool area, catching sight of the tall, pretty blonde she and Eddy had met with months ago. With her wavy hair blowing in the light breeze, Emily waved Kaylee over, a bright smile on her face.

Wet children speed-walked past Kaylee while adults sunbathed poolside or splashed in the lazy indoor/outdoor river. Kaylee made it to the rustic round table with cushioned chairs where Emily stood, and shook her hand. "Good to see you again."

Emily gestured for her to sit. "Would you like anything to drink?"

Kaylee sat in one of the chairs. "I'm fine, thank you."

Pictures of Club Tahoe were splayed across the table, causing Kaylee's pulse to race. Lighting and cake choices were a few of the decisions she'd put off, among many others.

Emily followed Kaylee's gaze. "I brought images from past parties to see if anything catches your eye."

Pinpricks snaked across Kaylee's skin. None of this felt right, but she attempted to hold a smile.

Emily spread out the pictures. "The Club Tahoe wedding coordinator will go through all of this and more, but due to the general size of your wedding, I wanted to make sure you were thinking of these things ahead of time. The deadlines are fast approaching, and I didn't want you to make a last-minute decision you weren't happy with." Emily smiled hesitantly. "You're a little behind on finalizing the layout and approximate guest numbers. Not that we need exact numbers just yet...but a sense of how many people you anticipate would be good."

Kaylee squeezed her hands in her lap. She couldn't do this. "Emily, can I ask you something? In confidence?"

God, was she seriously going to talk about her relationship drama with a near stranger? On the other hand, since they didn't know each other well, anything Kaylee said wasn't likely to go far.

Emily swallowed, a shaky smile crossing her face. "Yes. Anything."

"If we... That is to say, if Eddy and I were to cancel the wedding for some reason, what would happen to our contract?"

Emily let out a light breath. "If you think that's a possibility, you'd want to give the club notice within the next week. We can refund up to seventy-five percent of your deposit. Most places ask for more, but Club Tahoe is in high demand and we have a long waitlist." Her gaze grew concerned. "Is that something you think will happen?"

"I don't know."

Emily rested her hands on top of the table. "Kaylee, I feel I should say something." She pressed her lips together. "I was with Wes Cade and his brothers in the club lounge a few weeks ago. Wes said you two used to date?"

"We did. A long time ago."

She nodded stiffly. "While I was with the guys, we saw Eddy at the bar with some of his friends." She winced. "Has Wes said anything about that?"

Kaylee's breath locked in her chest. "He did, but he didn't go into details. He said... Eddy cheated." Repeating the words gave them substance—a palpability she hadn't been able to fully acknowledge until now. "Wes and I have a rocky past. I wasn't sure if I should believe him." She pressed her fingers to her eyes, then dropped her hands and gazed pleadingly at Emily. "What happened?"

Emily's mouth twisted to the side as though she were annoyed. Or disgusted. "Eddy left the lounge with a woman. When they returned, it looked like something had happened. Eddy had been touching the woman in a familiar way before they left the room. When they came back, his appearance—"

"Oh God." Kaylee sank her head to the table. Then she remembered where she was.

She stood abruptly. "I have to go. Can—can we finish another time?"

"Certainly." Emily stood and wrung her hands. "I'm so sorry. Please let me know if there's anything I can do. I just... I thought you should know."

"I— Thank you." Kaylee grabbed her purse and rushed out of the pool area, her bag falling halfway down her arm and catching on her legs. Her head pounded like it might explode.

How could she be so blind? This entire time, everyone knew Eddy was an ass. Except for her.

Wes knew.

Nausea rolled through her body as she darted across the lobby—where Wes, of all people, stood, talking to his youngest brother, Hunt.

Naturally Wes would be here to witness her humiliation.

He scanned her face, his brow furrowing. "What's wrong?"

Kaylee swept past him. No way could she talk to him right now. Not after what Emily had said.

Not after what Kaylee had finally realized.

Yes, she'd talked to Eddy and strongly suspected things. And yes, Wes had told her Eddy cheated, but not with any detail. Somehow the details were important. They made it real. And God, the details. It didn't take much for Kaylee's imagination to fill in the blanks Emily had left.

This was Kaylee's fault. Not Eddy's cheating, but where she was right now. Alone. Undervalued. Engaged to a man who wasn't faithful.

She'd agreed to a life with Eddy, because she was damaged and thought only Eddy could love her.

But Eddy was an ass, and her head was clear. She couldn't ever have kids, but she deserved a good guy. Not some jerk who manipulated her.

CHAPTER NINE

K aylee had two nights to compose herself before Eddy came home. But all that went to crap the moment his car pulled up the driveway.

After receiving a text from him that his plane had landed at the South Lake Tahoe airport, she'd gone outside and waited on the front steps. The drive from the airport to her parents' place was short, and she'd needed the fresh air.

But instead of remaining calm, as soon as he opened the car door, she blurted, "What happened with the woman inside Club Tahoe's lounge?"

Smooth. Nice way to confront your fiancé.

Eddy had been smiling when he saw her, but his smile died a quick death.

He reached across the seat and grabbed his briefcase, then stepped out of the car and shut the car door behind him. "What's going on, Kaylee? You've never been the jealous type. I don't like having to justify my every step."

She stood and crossed her arms as he approached. "Not your every step. Just the one night. I'm assuming it was the night before you left town?" He started to move past her, and she threw her arm out. "Answer the question, Eddy."

He let out a harsh sigh. "Really? We're going to do this now? I haven't even taken off my jacket."

She held his stare, and his gaze flickered away. "If you really want to know, women sometimes throw themselves at me. It happens to a lot of guys. But I'm committed to *you*. I want to build a life with you." He tried to reach for her, and she stepped back.

"Did. You. Touch. Her."

"Maybe." He tugged at his collar and ran a finger between the fabric and his skin. "I can't remember. We'd been drinking. Either way, she was all over me."

"Did you walk outside with her?"

His gaze darted to the side. "No, never."

Kaylee fell back a step. He was lying. The bastard. "*Get out.*"

"What?" A flash of desperation filled his eyes. "Kaylee, don't be stupid."

Stupid? Yeah, she'd been stupid. Believing Eddy. "You're lying. Even if I couldn't read it on your face, people *saw* you. They told me what happened."

His nostrils flared. "Who the fuck..." He shook his head and attempted to smile, but it was too late. She'd seen the anger in his eyes—because he'd been caught. "It doesn't matter what anyone says. So I talked to another woman. Big deal. You're not perfect either. I've seen the way you look at your golf instructor. You can't tell me nothing's going on there."

She swallowed, her throat the consistency of cardboard. "Actually, I can. I know Wes from college, but we don't have a physical relationship."

"I bet it was him," Eddy snarled. "He's the one filling

your head with lies. You trust that guy over your own fiancé? You're the one who doesn't know about commitment. I've been there for you. I'm the one who wants you, even though you'll never be able to give me a kid." He scanned her body in disgust.

Kaylee's mouth parted in shock. He'd never been so cruel. But then, he'd been lying about everything, hadn't he?

Eddy was sterile. He couldn't have children either, regardless of her infertility. What he said was nonsense. "Wes is a friend from my past. We dated in college, but there's nothing going on between us."

"Yeah, right. How many times have you fucked him?"

She shook her head. "I can't believe I ever agreed to marry you."

She grabbed the purse she'd brought onto the steps and pulled out her keys. She'd already set the flashy engagement ring he'd given her on the nightstand where he'd find it. Good thing too, or she might have thrown it at him. "The wedding is off. Grab your things and be out of my house within the hour." She pinned him with a glare. She'd never wanted to hit anyone before, but she wanted to hit Eddy. "If you're still here when I return, I'm calling the police."

Kaylee didn't know what the police could do. It wasn't like Eddy had committed a crime. But *she* might commit murder if he was still here when she got back.

Eddy's face turned a mottled red, his hands clenched into fists. For a moment, she feared he'd run after her. "The place in San Francisco is mine. Had it put in my name. If you leave me, you'll be homeless. You have no friends. And that golf pro is going to dump you once he finds out you're a bag of tits with no oven."

Kaylee glanced at the beautiful woods and the house

that she loved so much. "Better here than anywhere near you."

Eddy flung his briefcase at the side of the house. "Fucking barren bitch. You'll regret this!"

Kaylee spun and hurried to her car. She opened the door and lunged inside, fumbling with the keys. When the ignition turned over, she tore out of the driveway.

A mile down the main road, she pulled over and leaned across the seats, head out the passenger-side door. She heaved onto the side of the road. Nothing came up because she hadn't eaten since yesterday, but that didn't stop her stomach from roiling.

Another violent retch stole her breath and she gasped, tears streaming down her face. Eddy was the man she'd promised to share her life with. He was horrible, and she'd chosen him. That piece of shit.

Maybe if she hadn't been running so fast from her past, she wouldn't have jumped into the arms of a pathological liar.

———

WES SCRATCHED HIS NECK FORCEFULLY. "Son of a bitch."

He tossed his club in his golf bag and hauled it onto his shoulder. He'd practiced at the crack of dawn, like he'd been doing every day these last two months, then put in a few hours of lessons with clients. Afterward, it was back to the range for another two hours of practice. He would have stayed past dark, putting and chipping and honing his skills for the qualifying tournament, but Kaylee hadn't shown for her lesson this afternoon.

Wes had told Kaylee he didn't want to see her again, but

he hadn't actually believed she'd stay away. She was having her wedding at his goddamned resort, after all. And then he'd seen her crying on her way out of the lobby yesterday.

Wes strode to the pro shop and lifted his chin at the cashier. "I'm heading out." He set his golf bag behind the counter. "Close up tonight."

The twenty-year-old cashier saluted Wes and went back to eating his energy bar.

The shop and course were slow this afternoon. And in general. Wes would have to do something about that. Find a way to make it more profitable for the club and help his brothers preserve their father's legacy. But all of that could wait. At least for the rest of the evening.

Because Wes was heading out to find Kaylee.

Goddammit. Kaylee had caught him unawares, showing up at his club after four years. All he'd wanted was to discover her secrets and scoot her the hell out of his life. And here he was, going after her because she *wasn't* around.

Kaylee had been upset yesterday. Given the information he had on her fiancé... Wes needed to know she was okay.

Because he was worried.

He hated that he was worried about his ex, but she wasn't much of a crier. Kaylee was independent and chill most of the time, which was one of the things that had drawn him to her. She only cracked when deep shit went down. Like when they'd broken up.

So if she'd been crying yesterday and hadn't shown today, when she never missed a lesson before, something was off. That was the reason he hopped into his car and headed for her parents' cabin, cursing himself the entire way.

He should turn around. Go back. Thank his lucky stars she was staying away and move on with his life. But things still felt unfinished between them.

And he needed his mind cleared of anything having to do with Kaylee if he had any chance of making it through the qualifying rounds coming up.

CHAPTER TEN

Wes pulled up to Kaylee's parents' place for the first time in years. It looked exactly the same. Stone, with a rough wooden exterior sealed to keep the deep brown color intact. And there was only one car in the driveway.

Thank fuck her fiancé wasn't here. He would have a hard time explaining why a golf instructor needed to visit a client's home.

Wes exited the car and leapt up the porch steps two at a time, then knocked none too gently on the front door.

He'd make this brief. Find out why she hadn't shown and see if this was going to be the norm. That way he wouldn't always be looking over his shoulder, expecting his ex to come walking around the corner. He'd even help her find a new instructor.

That was the plan, anyway. Until she opened the door.

Kaylee was beautiful, as usual. Dressed casual. She wore no makeup, but she'd never needed it to look pretty. It was the look of the dead on her face that scared the shit out of him. "Hey."

She swallowed, her distant gaze locking on his eyes. "Wes? What are you doing here?"

He stepped inside without her offering, but she didn't protest.

Kaylee glanced to the side as though just noticing her surroundings.

Man, she was out of it. "You didn't show for your lesson. Bella was worried."

A lie. Bella had asked about Kaylee, but Wes was the one who worried. The pale cast to her face, her shaky frame, and the desolate look in her eyes told him he was right to come here.

She walked slowly across the room and sat on the couch, where a dent in the cushion suggested she'd been sitting for a good long while. "You told me to find a new instructor. I'm also not feeling well." Her voice came out scratchy, and she lifted her delicate fingers to her throat.

He hadn't planned on getting angry the other day. But his frustration had gotten the best of him. He'd been a dick, actually.

Maybe he had a right to his frustration. He didn't know anymore. He just knew he cared about Kaylee more than he did his reasons for being angry.

Wes stuffed his hands in the pockets of his khakis. "You should see a doctor. You don't seem well."

She studied his face.

He shifted his feet, finding it difficult to come across at ease. He was showing some of his cards, but he wasn't changing course now. Kaylee wasn't a bad person. It was okay to care, he told himself, justifying the visit.

She tucked her short, dark hair behind her ears. "I'm not sick."

He watched her shaky hand drop into her lap. "*Riiight.* When did you last eat?"

She sighed, her chest falling as though a bag of sand held it down. "Wes, why are you here?"

He noticed she didn't answer his question. "I told you. You didn't show for your lesson. The last time I saw you, you looked like you were about to hurl your lunch."

He didn't want to say exactly why he'd felt compelled to check in on her. That somewhere deep in his dark, cold heart, he still felt something for her, much as he wished it weren't true.

Recognition dawned on her face. "Right. I'd just spoken to Emily." She sank her head into her hands and mumbled something he couldn't hear.

"What was that?"

She looked up. "The wedding is off."

He let out a deep sigh. *Thank fuck.* "Are you okay?"

"I know you didn't like Eddy. You don't have to act all concerned."

He sat on the couch beside her, leaving a good two feet between them. "I wasn't a fan of McDouche...ah, Eddy. But I didn't intend to ruin your relationship with him. When we last talked...the things I said...they didn't come out right. Shit, I didn't even know I was going to say them. I thought I'd let you figure it out on your own. But then you mentioned trust... I got defensive. Shouldn't have taken out my anger that way."

Her mouth curved up. "I didn't exactly believe you, if that makes you feel any better."

For a moment, his heart sped at the teasing look in her eye. And then he took in her words.

His shoulders tensed. "Why would you believe me? Oh,

wait. *Maybe because I've never lied to you.* Not all men are like Eddy."

She frowned. "You might not have lied to me, but you hurt me."

"*I* hurt *you?* Other way around, Kaylee."

He scrubbed a hand down his face. Rehashing the same old argument wasn't why he'd come here. "If I hurt you in the past, it wasn't intentional. And I wasn't trying to hurt you again the other day. Nor did I come here to upset you. I came to check in." He glanced down her body. "You look shaky and you've got dark circles under your eyes."

"Thanks for pointing out how bad I look."

He frowned, but it was halfhearted. She never did let him get away with anything—and he liked that about her. "That's not what I meant."

She leaned back and hugged a couch pillow. "Sorry. I know you're here because... Actually, I'm not sure why you're here. But I'm fine. Really."

He hated that she was closed off to him now. "Have you eaten? How about I make you something?"

Her forehead scrunched and then she laughed—and it was melodic and pretty and genuine. Just like the girl he remembered. "Since when do you cook?"

He rolled his eyes. "A man can't live on frozen food alone. I've learned a few things."

Not exactly true. He wasn't much of a cook, which was why he went to Adam's place when he felt like eating something decent. His brother kicked ass in the kitchen. Adam's fiancée Hayden might not be a fan of Wes showing up unannounced, but what were brothers for?

That glassy, desolate look crossed her eyes again. "I'm not hungry, Wes."

He studied her for a moment, then stood. "You mind if I

grab something? You may not be hungry, but I am. Spent a long day practicing."

She flopped back and stared at the ceiling. "Have at it."

Wes checked the cupboards and fridge. Not much in the house, but he found what he was searching for. He pulled out a bag of microwave popcorn and butter.

He might not be a cook, but he was a master at timing the microwave popcorn to perfection before half the bag burned. That technical expertise came from experience.

Wes placed the bag in the microwave, cut the stick of butter in half, and dropped it in a small bowl. Rummaging through a few more cupboards, he found a larger bowl, and grabbed that one as well.

When the popcorn was ready, Wes pulled it out of the microwave and opened the bag—without scalding his face—and poured it in the large bowl.

He shoved the butter in the microwave and nuked it for a few seconds, making sure it was nice and melted.

Kaylee frowned. "Popcorn? Anything else I can get you? Maybe a home-cooked meal?"

"You offering? Because I sure as shit won't pass that up. Don't pretend."

Her look was pure exasperation. "No, I'm not offering. My life is crumbling and you're eating all my food."

"It's only popcorn." The microwave beeped and Wes pulled out the butter and poured it over the food in question. "And if you're not going to eat it, why should I let it go to waste?"

"Isn't there somewhere you need to be? The pro shop? Teaching Bella, maybe?"

"Nope." He returned to the couch, closer this time, allowing the steam from the popcorn to waft in her direction. He jammed his hand in the bowl and shoved the buttery goodness in his mouth.

She watched him with a look of disgust on her face that he didn't believe for one second.

"Mmm. Good stuff. You want any?" He offered her the bowl.

She looked away. "No."

After a few moments, during which the only sounds permeating the room consisted of Wes crunching on popcorn, Kaylee twisted toward him. "Why didn't you like him?"

He assumed this was about McDouche. "He wasn't good enough for you."

"He was a good boyfriend," she said, but even Wes could hear the lack of conviction in her tone.

He raised an eyebrow.

"Fine, he was a lying asshole. Is that what you wanted to hear?"

"If it fits."

She absently reached over and grabbed a handful of popcorn, eating it while she spoke. "I didn't know he was lying. I had no reason not to trust him."

"Sure you didn't. You'd just come out of a relationship where the man you were with was *honest*. You had no experience with lying bastards."

Her mouth twisted. "I hope you're not referring to yourself. I hate to tell you, but you were not a paragon."

He gestured to his chest in mock disbelief while she stole another handful of popcorn. Which had been his intent all along—to get her to eat. Asking her to eat would get him nowhere. She was beautiful *and* stubborn.

A stab of something hit Wes in the chest. Nostalgia? Fuck, he didn't know, but he brushed it off. Didn't need that shit clouding his judgment right now. "You have to admit, I never lied to you. I wasn't perfect, but I loved you." A prickle of unease shot through him. He was exposing himself.

He sensed her stare and cleared his throat. "Anyway, you never explained what I did that was so horrible and made me *an absent boyfriend.* Most women give their guys the courtesy of telling them what they've done wrong before dumping their asses."

Kaylee extended her arm for another handful of popcorn, and Wes pulled the bowl out of reach.

She glared. "I thought you were here to make me feel better? Share, dammit."

He narrowed his eyes, but his chest heated. This was why he'd loved Kaylee. She was stubborn, feisty, and territorial over food. He respected the hell out of her. "I came to check on you, not cheer you up. No more food until you tell me what you're keeping behind lock and key inside that head of yours."

She looked away and brushed her hands together, knocking off popcorn flakes. "I can't."

"Can't or won't?"

"It's hard for me, Wes. Really hard. I'm scared."

She was serious. Obviously. Whatever this was about had destroyed their relationship. He'd thought she'd gotten sick of him putting her on the back burner for his golf career —and that might have been part of it—but there was more. And he'd only recently realized it.

He'd been so pissed that she'd dumped him and his career had tanked, he'd never considered there might be another reason behind their breakup.

Would it change anything? Probably not, but he still wanted to know what she was keeping from him.

"I can't talk about it right now," she continued. "I'm in an emotional wasteland. Bringing up the past... I just can't go there."

"Fair enough." He gave her the bowl, but she didn't dig in. She looked crushed. "You should come to your next lesson."

"Why? I'm not with Eddy anymore. I don't need to practice for our honeymoon. There is no stupid honeymoon. And you're not teaching me, remember?" She set the bowl on the side table with a loud thunk.

"You said he wasn't the only reason you were taking lessons."

"He's not...but I feel like crap. I can't go out right now. Maybe in a few weeks."

"All the more reason for you to show up. And not in a few weeks; that's not healthy."

He mentally shook his head. Since when was he the mental health expert? He'd spent the last four years being angry over his ex dumping him.

Wes stood and grabbed one last fistful of popcorn. "And eat some food, Kaylee. Don't make me come over and cook more popcorn. We'll tap out on my food prep skills real quick."

She tried to hide a smile. "Wouldn't want that." She let out a deep sigh. "Thank you, though. For coming today."

He crunched on the popcorn. "Only came because you didn't show," he said around a mouthful of food. "Pisses me off when my clients miss appointments. It's rude."

She smiled. "So you're my instructor again?"

He shrugged noncommittally.

"Fine," she said, and sank back into the couch cushions. "I'll be there."

CHAPTER ELEVEN

Kaylee made a quick trip home to her folks' house and shared the news about her broken engagement. And swung by her family doctor to get tested for STDs, because *eww*. She didn't know if Eddy had practiced safe sex. Somehow, Kaylee doubted it. At least her doctor told her she was in the clear. She supposed that was some consolation.

Her parents didn't seem surprised about the split. In fact, her father appeared downright pleased.

How could she have been so blind? Who knew how many women Eddy had slept with while they were together? Now that she saw the real Eddy, she couldn't unsee what a disgusting human being he was. Apparently, when you were running from ghosts, you made terrible decisions. Like spending your life with a guy because he couldn't have children either.

To make matters worse, Eddy phoned in some misguided attempt at getting back together and accused *her* of being the problem.

Oh, hell no. She wasn't walking around in a daze

anymore. That call had lasted all of two seconds, before she told him to never reach out to her again.

Kaylee made it to her next golf lesson, and no, she wasn't happy. She felt like crap, but Wes was right. She couldn't mope around and not take care of herself.

Wes didn't ask any questions about the breakup, just nodded his approval at her being there, and proceeded to make her sweat it out at the driving range for a couple of hours. Which, in some weird way, made her feel better, because it took her mind off the rest of her life.

Wes, like Kaylee and Bella, was in training mode. He practiced alongside them and was hyper-focused, just as he'd been in college. Kaylee wondered why he was practicing so hard. It reminded her of their painful past together.

If Kaylee really wanted to depress herself, she thought about how she'd come full circle—hanging out with Wes, attracted to him, as always, but never his priority. She was *not* interested in dating Wes or anyone right now. Was it even possible to rebound with the ex you rebounded from? That was a hell of a mindbender. No, when she was ready, she would move forward, not backward. And good God, dating Wes would be taking five steps back.

Kaylee had other things on her mind, anyway, like where to live. Eddy had somehow stolen the apartment she'd rented in San Francisco, and she couldn't care less. A year ago, he had insisted on buying all new furniture, so the only things she'd left behind were a few clothes and some knickknacks her father had graciously offered to pick up so that she wouldn't have to deal with Eddy. Moving back to the city would feel like stepping back, and if she was making a fresh start, she wanted it to be somewhere she could see herself living long term.

After practice, Kaylee went into emergency get-your-life-back-on-track mode. Tapping her pen at the makeshift desk she'd set up at the kitchen table, she sifted through Craigslist, Monster.com, and other job search engines, and filled out job applications. The jobs she found didn't pay much, but she wanted something she might enjoy. For now, she only needed enough money to survive on. Her parents' place was paid for, and they said she could stay as long as she liked.

Despite the massive turn her life had taken, she felt surprisingly Zen with everything. As though a weight had been lifted. And maybe it had. Somehow, things would be okay. As long as she didn't forget the boundaries that needed to remain between her and Wes.

———

WES SCANNED the applicants in his inbox for the new assistant golf pro position. Very few people had experience with children. He could hire someone without it. Their new direct marketing was working better than expected, and they needed instructors for adults too. But Bella had changed Wes's opinion on the whole "training kids" thing.

When Emily had first approached him about giving a spunky five-year-old golf lessons, he'd nearly run from the room. Then she'd explained Bella's situation. And how often Bella's parents came to the club.

The little girl was ignored and bored. Wes could relate. He'd been that bored kid, hanging out at the club while he mourned the loss of his mother. Instead of spending time with his five young sons, Wes's father had buried himself in work. Wes had always hated that his father had chosen the club over him.

He had agreed to one lesson with Bella. Until he saw her skills and determination.

Bella's swing had been all over the place, like most new players. But she had an amazing ability to watch Wes and repeat the form he showed her. He'd seen real potential there. And that had excited him. The more he worked with Bella, the more he believed she could become a great golfer one day.

At first, it irritated Wes that Bella's parents were such selfish assholes that they couldn't be bothered to spend time with their daughter. But he changed his mind when he decided to train Bella as his protégée. Let her parents do their thing; he'd make sure Bella kicked ass at golf.

It didn't take long before Wes was rethinking the children's program Emily had been begging him to extend to the golf program. If even half of the kids who took lessons at the course had Bella's energy for the game, it would be worth it. In fact, he liked the idea of training the next generation. Made him feel like he was doing something important.

Wes scanned the list of applicants again. He wrote down the phone numbers of those experienced with children. Anyone he hired would go through a full screening, but a background working with kids suddenly seemed essential.

He shut down his computer and stood, ready to put in another three hours on the practice green. He'd given an extra lesson to Kaylee earlier in the day after she'd called to see if he had time. He usually worked on his short game then, but he couldn't say no. She was going through a lot, and no matter how screwed up their past was, he wouldn't leave her hanging.

She'd shown up in fitted red golf shorts and a white

polo, and it was good to see color in her face. Some of her energy was back, and he'd not gone easy on her.

Wes smiled, remembering Kaylee's disgruntled look when he told her to grab another bucket of balls ten minutes before her lesson was supposed to wrap up. He'd made her stay until she emptied it. By the end, her cotton polo shirt stuck to her petite frame, and she was out of breath. Which Wes took to mean that he'd done a good job. No one should leave his lessons without a few muscles burning.

On that note, he'd better get his ass on the practice green before it got too dark to see the balls. He grabbed his clubs and shoved his phone in his navy-blue golf pants, right as the thing vibrated.

Wes dug his hand in his pocket and fished out the phone. "Hello," he said, locking up his office and scanning the pro shop to make sure his staff had shut it down properly.

"Wes, it's Tom."

"Hey, man. How are things in SF?" Tom Henderson was a buddy of Wes's who'd made it onto the pro tour straight out of college. Pretty much Wes's one and only dream in life. Until Kaylee had kicked him to the curb and made a head case out of him. And now she was back in his life. Which had to be some sort of sick twist of fate. It didn't help that he still found her attractive, even when she was sweaty after a grueling golf lesson. *Especially* when she was sweaty.

Wes hadn't been with a woman since Kaylee arrived. He'd blamed it on his rigorous training schedule, but he worried it was more than that.

"Wes, I gotta catch a flight, but there's something that came up," Tom said, cutting into Wes's daydream of removing Kaylee's sweaty shirt for her. "One of the courses on the tour had an accident. Major fire at the clubhouse. No one got hurt, but the place won't be repaired in time for the tournament. The tour needs a replacement."

Wes froze in the act of turning off the lights in the pro shop, and then his heart hammered in his chest.

It was extremely rare for a disaster to bump a course from the tour. "*Please* tell me Club Tahoe is being considered. And if you're messing with me, I will hunt you down."

Tom laughed. "Yeah, buddy. I happened to be in the right place at the right time and boasted about your course. Didn't hurt that one of the panel members has played there."

"Are you shitting me?" Wes paced the room, running a hand roughly through his hair.

He dumped his clubs near the front counter. This was the opportunity of a lifetime for the resort, which had taken a hit financially since he and his brothers began running it.

None of his brothers had wanted anything to do with the resort once they were adults. Had, in fact, run from it. His brother Adam was the exception. Adam had worked for their father and ended up an executive at Blue Casino. Wes was somewhat of an exception too, but only because he liked the golf course. His other three brothers had worked blue-collar jobs prior to their father's death. They hadn't known jack about running a luxury resort, and had been stumbling to catch up ever since.

"I'm not shitting you, but you need to act fast. I pitched Club Tahoe and they were receptive, but you've got to jump on it." Tom rattled off the name and number of the person in charge.

Wes lunged across the front counter for a pen and scribbled down the information.

"Tell them I referred you and that your course will be ready in time for the tournament."

"Yeah, anything. Which tournament is it?"

"Second of the season."

Wes did a quick mental calculation. "That's in seven weeks."

"Yep. You still want it?"

Wes would be a fool to pass up the opportunity. "Hell yes."

"Then make that call. I'll be in touch when I return to San Francisco. Oh, and Wes?"

"Yeah—I'm here." Which he was, even if his mind was running a mile a minute.

"Don't forget, if the tourney takes place at Club Tahoe, the club pro gets one of the sponsor's exemptions."

During Wes's mental rundown of all the things he'd need to do to get the course ready for a tournament, and that was assuming the tour chose Club Tahoe as the replacement course, he'd skipped over one very important bonus.

As the club's head pro, he could play in the tournament. Without the need to qualify.

Holy fucking shit.

Wes somehow managed to end the call without passing out. He placed his hands on the counter and took a deep breath.

This could change everything. The direction of the club. The direction of his golf career.

CHAPTER TWELVE

Wes swung open the door to Levi's office the next morning and stormed inside. "Brace yourself."

Emily scrambled off Levi's lap, clutching her top together and buttoning it.

Wes covered his eyes. "Sorry—should have knocked."

"Asshole," Levi grumbled. "My girlfriend works here. What do you think we do when no one's around?"

Wes peeked to make sure the coast was clear, then dropped his hand. "Work?"

"No, shithead, we make out...and other stuff." Levi said that last bit under his breath. Emily covered her flushed face with her hand and shook her head. Levi pointed at Wes. "So keep that in mind before you come barging in here."

Wes rolled his eyes. "Good job, Levi. Real professional."

"Don't listen to him," Emily said. "We don't make out *all* day."

"Would if I could," Levi mumbled.

Emily picked up paperwork from the corner of Levi's desk. "I'll go. Give you guys some space."

Levi grabbed her hand and tugged her back onto his lap. "Stay."

Wes closed the door behind him. "Actually, Emily, I need you here for this. What I have to say is huge—all hands on deck."

As soon as Wes had stopped repeating the words *sponsor's exemption* five hundred times in his head, with visions of holding a trophy, he pulled it together and spoke to Tom's tournament contact. The manager was completely on board with the switch to Club Tahoe—and had even agreed to change the tournament's name. As long as Wes could prepare the course and facility in time.

"We're hosting the Tahoe Invitational." Wes rose on the balls of his feet, his body vibrating with excitement.

Levi looked at Emily. "Do you know what he's talking about?"

She shook her head, but her eyes glowed. Emily was a sharp one. Wes could see her mentally putting the pieces together. "Are you talking about a professional tournament? Coming here?"

"Yes, motherfuckers. *Yes.*" Wes clapped his hands loudly and strode across the room. He sat on the edge of Levi's desk, eliciting a frown from his brother.

Emily stood—despite Levi's grabby hands—and walked over, tapping on her tablet as though she were searching for a screen to take notes. "When?" she said. "And what are we talking about in terms of people to accommodate?"

"Not people. *Crowds.*" Wes turned to Levi. "Are you even listening?" Levi was staring at Emily as though he were considering pulling her back on his lap. "Do you know what this means for the club?"

His brother scratched his jaw. "Does this have to do

with your buddy Tom? I don't trust anything that comes out of that jackass's mouth."

The one and only time Wes had coordinated a meeting between his brother and Tom, Wes and Tom had gotten hammered and taken women home instead of talking about bringing a tourney to the club. And okay, that had been an immature thing to do, but that was months ago. Wes had had his fill of stupid shit like that. He wanted more.

And his vision of success had just landed in his lap.

"Forget all that. This isn't a chance opportunity; it's the real deal. I signed the preliminary contract this morning." Wes placed a sheet in front of Levi.

Levi stared at the document. "Without my permission?"

"The final version will need to be signed off by all of us. I figured you'd want me to handle the course details."

"You thought right." Levi tapped his finger on his desk. "What else is involved? Can we even handle something this big? When is it exactly, anyway?"

"Seven weeks, which is why they gave it to us. I promised we'd be ready."

"Seven weeks?" Levi bellowed. "Have you lost your mind?"

Wes rubbed his chin. "It'll be a miracle if we pull it off. But if we do? Our resort will be in the world's spotlight. Think about it, Levi. We could become a regular stop on the tour. And this tourney will ensure full hotel booking during the event at a premium price. But if we're going to make this work, it'll require every single employee busting their ass. We'll need to hire additional personnel, no question..." Wes stood and paced, then stopped abruptly and stared at Levi. "Fuck. Can we do this?"

Emily tapped feverishly on her tablet, taking down notes or calculating—who knew what she did on that thing?

"Yes. Yes, we can. If we hire a boatload of temporary employees and make sure our existing services are running like a machine. The only program that isn't is Club Kids. We've got it booked out, with more guests requesting it every day, so we don't want to screw it up. But if I find someone amazing to run the program, we should be fine."

Levi rubbed his mouth. "We've been using our regular crew to bolster Club Kids, but that won't work during the tournament. How soon can you hire a full-time manager for it?"

Emily bit her lip. "Depends on the candidates that apply. It's kids; there's no way I'll hire just anyone. I need someone totally trustworthy and hands-on. Someone who will jump in and make the program great."

Levi sighed. "So basically, we need a miracle worker to fall in our laps."

Emily nodded slowly. "Pretty much. But let me get the word out and see what I can come up with. I'll post the job description this afternoon. Sometimes it takes forever to fill a position, and sometimes I luck out and land someone on the first try."

"While you're doing that," Wes said, "I'll put together a meeting with my staff. The tour must offer support. I'll look into what all that entails, as well as specific requirements for security, hospitality, vending... *Shit*, the list is long, isn't it?" Wes started pacing again. "Levi, now would be a good time to reach out to that lawyer you hired and make sure the contract I signed is solid."

"On it." Levi picked up the document. "I'll get the finance director and Jared in here too. They'll need to know what's going on."

"Right." Wes scrunched his face up. "Still can't believe you hired your ex's boyfriend."

"Hey," Emily said indignantly. "Jared is awesome. And Lisa isn't only Levi's ex, she's my sister, which trumps ex classifications."

Wes gave her a blank stare. "Emily, don't use convoluted female logic on me right now. Kaylee's messed with my head enough these last few weeks."

He moved toward the door. "Levi, call in our brothers, yeah? Let them know what's on the horizon and to get their asses in gear. For the next few weeks, I'll be tied up at the course, getting things arranged. I'm leaving it up to you two to handle the resort portion."

"Sure, just leave us the resort." Levi flashed Wes a look of annoyance, but he turned toward his computer and started typing out what appeared to be an email, his broad shoulders and bulky arms hunched to accommodate the narrow keyboard.

Levi used to be a fireman, until he got injured. Seeing his blue-collared, muscular brother behind a desk—and kicking ass—was shocking and funny as hell to Wes. But all of his brothers had been forced to step out of their comfort zones after their father died.

"You want the golf course?" Wes said. "'Cause I'd love to see you try and take on that one."

Levi flipped him the bird. "Get out of here so I can work."

Wes hurried out of Levi's office, his head buzzing with excitement and trepidation. Fucking hell, this was intense. He didn't know if they'd pull it off, but he was going to do everything in his power to try. Because this opportunity wasn't only for him, it was for his brothers as well.

———

KAYLEE PASSED the Club Tahoe front desk and turned left down a long corridor that ended in a double door. She entered the executive offices, and shivers ran down her body. This was the final step in canceling her wedding. It wasn't that this was the wrong thing. It was simply one of those steps that propelled her life in a totally different direction. Uncharted and scary.

She took a deep breath and spoke to the male receptionist at the entrance. He confirmed her appointment and asked her to have a seat.

Kaylee eased into one of the upholstered reception chairs and twined her fingers together, her knuckles bleaching white.

"Kaylee?"

She glanced up to see Emily standing in front of one of the offices, a kind smile on her face.

"Come on in." She gestured toward the door.

Kaylee stood and walked down the hallway, passing several workers bustling about. The employees seemed busier than the last time she'd ventured to these offices. With Eddy. *Ugh.* This was the right move, but it didn't help to think about the monumental mistake she'd almost made. And to contemplate starting her life over from scratch.

"Thank you for meeting with me today," she said once Emily had closed the door to her office. "I didn't realize it would be so busy this late in the afternoon."

Emily sighed and sat behind her desk. "Normally, it's not. But we just received notice we'll be hosting a professional golf tournament in under two months."

Despite where Kaylee's life was, she could appreciate how awesome that news must be for the club. And for Wes. "That's amazing. Congratulations. Wes must be so excited."

"You know, I can't tell. I mean, yes, he seemed excited,

but it's pretty crazy what we need to do in order to get the resort ready."

"Well, don't let me take up your time. I just came by to sign the wedding cancellation forms."

Emily frowned. "I'm so sorry, Kaylee. I worried when I last saw you that this might happen."

"Thank you. I'm only sorry things got this far. It's complicated..."

Had she ever been in love with Eddy, or he with her? Right now, Kaylee second-guessed everything.

"No explanations necessary." Emily lifted an envelope from her desk and extended it to Kaylee with a gentle smile. "I spoke to Levi and we were able to give you the entire deposit back. It turns out we have a couple who would love to move up their wedding date."

"Oh, wow. Will you thank Levi for me?"

"I sure will." Emily's eyebrows knitted together. "How are you overall?"

"Better. I mean, I'm uprooted, but I feel more whole somehow, which is probably a sign that things weren't right. And I've decided to stay in town, though I need to find a job now... That's why I couldn't come earlier this afternoon. I've been interviewing all day." Kaylee frowned. "I forgot how small this town is. There isn't a lot available outside of gaming. Hopefully, I'll find something soon, because moving back in with my parents at the age of twenty-six is not appealing." She chuckled.

"No, of course not," Emily said slowly. "What kind of jobs are you looking at?"

"I majored in sociology with a minor in early childhood studies, and I used to work for a women and children's non-profit. So, aside from substitute teaching, I've found a few non-profits and one or two social programs that seemed interesting."

Emily sat forward. "*Really*. Well, you know, the club has a position we urgently need filled. It might not be a perfect fit, and the pay isn't much, but it relates to children. I don't suppose you'd be interested in applying to run our Club Kids program? It's growing exponentially, and we need someone trustworthy with good organizational skills. The pay will also increase after we get the program fully up and running."

Working at Club Tahoe hadn't been on Kaylee's radar. Wes probably wouldn't be happy about it... But she'd scoured the want ads for days and there really wasn't much out there. "I'd be very interested, actually."

"Wonderful." Emily beamed. She stood and handed Kaylee her business card. "Email me your résumé and we can go from there."

What should have been entirely disheartening—finalizing the end of her wedding—had turned out to be...oddly invigorating.

A job at the club?

Wes would hate it.

But Kaylee could think of worse places to work. Club Tahoe was paradise compared to some of the places she'd worked for in the past. And if she was supporting children, it wouldn't be bad at all. Not exactly what she had in mind for a career, but she only needed something to get her back on her feet.

CHAPTER THIRTEEN

"You hired who?" For a second, Wes thought Emily said she'd hired Kaylee to work at the club.

"You heard me right, Wes. And I don't want lip from you," Emily said from beside Levi's desk.

This time, Wes hadn't walked in on them unannounced. He'd learned his lesson the last time. He knocked first. But it wouldn't have mattered, because Levi and Emily were actually working when he came in.

"You aren't the only one scrambling to get the club ready for the tournament," she said. "We needed someone to run Club Kids, and Kaylee was the perfect candidate. In fact, she's way overqualified. But if all goes well, I'll be able to convince her to stay on. In the last two weeks, she's managed to pull together a program that was running on a shoestring budget. It goes without saying that the parents love her."

"Two weeks?" How the hell had he missed that? Oh yeah, he'd been busy putting together a tournament.

No doubt the parents loved Kaylee. On the surface, she was beautiful and sweet and gentle, with small things like children and puppies. But getting your heart crushed, even by soft hands, wasn't something a guy easily forgot.

Wes slid a look to Levi, who was smiling at Emily. "I see your velvet hammer is in full effect."

"You have no idea," Levi said proudly. "And if we manage to get the resort ready in time for the tournament, you can thank Emily for it."

Emily tapped on her tablet. "Not true. Everyone's been contributing." She peered lovingly at Levi. "Especially you."

"Because of that whip you've been wielding," Wes muttered.

Emily grinned. "I do like that part."

"Babe, don't take away all my thunder," Levi said. "You know how much I enjoy throwing my weight around here."

"And I need you to. That flaky chef is giving Bran a hard time again. Can you talk to him?"

"*Macon.*" Levi leaned back in his chair and crossed his thick arms over his chest. "It'd be my pleasure to make sure that pretty boy is doing his job. Matter of fact, maybe Bran should promote Macon's second-in-command. We're all tired of Macon's after-hours activities affecting his job."

"I couldn't agree more," Emily said, and switched out papers on Levi's desk. "Sign these, please. They need to go to finance."

Wes blinked and rubbed his forehead. The conversation had derailed. "Getting back to Kaylee, you really think it's a good idea for her to work here?"

"Yes," Emily said. "And it wouldn't hurt for you to check in on her. She's dealing with a major life change."

"She's my *ex*. Why would I check in on her?"

"Because you care about her?" Emily said sweetly.

Dammit, he did. But he didn't like his family knowing

it. And he didn't like the look in Emily's eyes when she brought up Kaylee. As though he and Kaylee might get back together—and that was never happening.

He cared about Kaylee, but she'd burned him. He had enough disappointments in his life without going through another round with his ex. Even if she was beautiful. And sweet and feisty, just like he liked his women.

Lately, however, he'd preferred the easy, uncomplicated type. Women he didn't care to go back to. And it had been over a month since he'd been with one of them...

Jesus, maybe it wasn't the tournament preparation that was frying his brain. All he needed was a good lay to cleanse the mental sludge that had taken shape in his overworked body and mind, compounded by too much interaction with his ex.

"I've seen her during lessons and she seems fine," he said. But Wes wasn't so sure. She'd been pretty messed up when he found her after Eddy McDouche had cheated on her.

"Listen." Emily actually set down her tablet. "I've invited Kaylee to drinks in the lounge with us tonight. We all missed it last week, and everyone could use a chance to unwind. If we don't, we'll be toast by the time the tournament arrives."

True. However... "Those regular get-togethers are for *the brothers*."

"And Emily," Levi said sharply.

"And I've invited Kaylee," Emily said. "She has no one in town, and I really like her. She's super sweet and very smart. And she's helped me a ton. You don't have to come if you don't want to, Wes, but Kaylee's invited."

Wes glared at Levi. "Since when do women come before brothers?"

Levi tugged Emily closer and wrapped his arm around her waist. "Emily is family. Get used to it."

Wes threw up his hands. "You're not even married. Adam has an excuse to bring Hayden to beer nights—they're engaged."

"It's only a matter of time," Levi said.

Emily blushed at the touching look Levi sent her.

This scene was enough to make Wes hurl. "I'm outta here." He headed for the door.

"You coming tonight?" Levi said.

Wes opened the door and glanced back. "I'll go, but don't think my habits are gonna change just because my ex is there. If she doesn't like seeing me hook up with other women, she can find different friends to hang out with."

"Giving yourself a lot of credit there, Wes," Emily said. "How do you know Kaylee even cares?"

Because *Wes* cared. But he wasn't going to admit that to these two.

"I just know." He swept out and down the hall.

Probably good for Kaylee to see him with other women. Would put them on the right footing moving forward if she was going to continue working at his resort.

———

"WHAT ABOUT THAT ONE?" Kaylee pointed across the lounge at a beautiful woman with red hair.

Wes gritted his teeth. This wasn't what he had in mind. Not. At. All.

Levi, the dumbass, had blurted that Wes was scouting women tonight, and Kaylee got the bright idea to help him out.

What. The. Fuck?

He glowered. "I don't need your help."

"I have very good taste in women. Not so much in men."

Considering she'd chosen *him* to date at one point, Wes ignored that comment.

Kaylee smiled prettily. "I can identify a psycho chick at one glance."

"What if I like psycho chicks?" No guy liked psycho chicks, but this conversation was getting out of hand and he'd say just about anything to get her to stop "helping" him.

She waved him off. "That's silly. The psycho ones end up stalking you and killing your cat when you're not looking."

"I don't own a cat." This was not how he'd envisioned beer with his brothers. This night was meant to relax him, not cause him more stress. "I can find my own woman, Kaylee." He smiled, but it might have come off a tad predatory, given her flinch.

He'd slept with a hell of a lot of women since their breakup. Not that he'd boast. It had been purely for survival and not because he was proud of it. Someday, he'd want a girlfriend again.

One who wasn't complicated.

Or prone to dumping a guy on his ass.

"Point is," he continued, "I got this, don't you worry."

But really, Kaylee picking out women had totally turned him off to the idea. He glared at his brothers, sitting around the table and taking in their conversation as though it were a sitcom.

"I don't know, Wes," Hunt said. "You should listen to Kaylee. I wouldn't mind having her for a wingman." Hunt's gaze slid down Kaylee's T-shirt, which clung lightly to her curves. She wasn't dressed up, but she didn't need to be. She was a beautiful woman, and Hunt was addicted to beautiful women.

Wes shot his brother a glare, and Hunt smirked, the jackass.

"That's wingwoman," Kaylee said, and grinned. "And I'd be happy to hook you up, Hunt."

Wes stared suspiciously at the drink in her hand. She was on beer number four, not that he was counting. But she'd also had a shot with Emily as a warm-up when they first arrived. If Wes recalled correctly, his ex would be three sheets to the wind if she didn't stop drinking.

Kaylee flagged the waitress and ordered a Long Island Iced Tea.

Good God, what was she trying to do? Drown herself?

He gestured at the drink the waitress brought her. "Maybe you should chill on that. I've seen what happens when you're drunk."

Kaylee's eyes narrowed. "I'm single, Wes. I don't have a keeper, and I'm not looking for one."

"You go, girl!" Emily high-fived Kaylee, but it was a drunken high five. They nearly missed, which caused the women to burst into laughter.

Wes looked at Levi.

"Don't glare at me," Levi said. "You think I have a say in these things?"

Fuck. Wes never thought he'd see the day his oldest brother became ball-shackled. "You disappoint me, you really do."

Levi's response was to nuzzle his girlfriend's neck. Meanwhile, Hunt already had a woman on his lap—where she came from, Wes hadn't a clue—and Adam stood to leave.

"I'm off," Adam said. "Hayden and I have plans to make. You all heard we pushed the wedding up?"

Bran tipped up the bill of his baseball cap. The rest of them had given up the stupid hats, but not Bran. If Bran didn't resemble him and his brothers so much, Wes would wonder whether Bran was of his blood. The guy could be a monk. "I thought the wedding wasn't until this spring?"

Adam glanced nervously at Kaylee. "It was...but with a cancellation in the schedule, we were able to move it forward." He looked apologetically at Kaylee. "I'm sorry. I hope that's okay."

Kaylee waved lazily—drunkenly. "Better you than me."

Club Tahoe booked weddings a year or more in advance, even in the fall and winter. Kaylee must have booked her wedding a year ago—and now that the slot was open, Adam and Hayden had snatched it.

She could pretend all she wanted, with the playful wingwoman crap, but considering the amount of alcohol she'd consumed tonight, Wes highly doubted Kaylee was over her broken engagement.

He didn't know why that bothered him, but it did.

CHAPTER FOURTEEN

Most of the time, Wes was a one-track guy when it came to prospecting hookups. But tonight he was distracted, because he saw things from a different perspective—a *woman* searching for a hookup.

Some piece of shit in a fancy suit was all over Kaylee, chatting her up. Wes didn't care what his and Kaylee's relationship status was—there was no way he'd let her go home with this guy while she was drunk.

If she was sober? Maybe.

Okay, he'd have issues with that too, but definitely not if she'd been drinking.

He stood and threw down some bills. "I'm out."

Bran was texting, Adam had left an hour ago, and Hunt had stolen out with the woman he'd had in his lap earlier.

Levi looked up from his conversation with Emily. "So soon?"

Wes knew what his brother was getting at. He hadn't picked up a woman yet, and he never went home alone when he was hellbent on finding one. But whatever. After the week he'd had making a million final arrangements for the tournament, he needed his bed more than a warm body. Bran must be rubbing off on him. And wasn't that a depressing thought? "I'll catch you tomorrow. Eight, right?"

Levi nodded. "We'll be here bright and early. Working through the weekends will be the norm until the Tahoe Invitational."

Wes nodded, his gaze snagging on Kaylee a few feet away. The guy had his hand on her hip, and Wes's muscles tensed.

Levi looked over as well. "We'll make sure she gets home okay."

"Don't bother," Wes said. "I got this." He strode over to Kaylee and did something he'd pay for later, but he didn't give a shit.

Wes snaked his arm around Kaylee's waist and toppled her back into his chest. "Babe, time to go."

She swiveled her head back, her gaze wavering as though she were at sea. "What?"

No way he'd leave her behind while she was this drunk, even with Levi's promise to watch out for her. He grabbed her hand and started pulling her away. Fortunately, she didn't pull back or try to stop him. The guy she'd been talking to complained, but Wes ignored him entirely.

"What's going on?" she asked.

He waited until they were in the lobby before he stopped and looked her in the eye. "I'm taking you home."

She laughed. "Let me get this straight. You can scout out women all night long, but I can't go home with a guy?" She crossed her arms and wobbled, but that didn't stop a stubborn look from settling onto her beautiful face. "I'm single, and I'm not your responsibility. I haven't been for a long time. I'm no one's responsibility." A hint of vulnerability tinged her tone.

"You're not going home with a guy while you're drunk." He didn't tell her he'd have dragged her away even if she weren't drunk. Because he couldn't explain that one.

"I'm a grown woman. You have no right—*no right!*" Her expression was indignant, but he sensed there was more to tonight's rebellion. She was hurting. Was it all because of McDouche? She'd nearly married the guy, but as far as Wes was concerned, Kaylee had dodged a landmine, getting out before it was too late.

He shoved his hands in his pockets and glanced away, letting out a stiff breath. "Do you really want to go home with a random dude?"

She swallowed, not meeting his eyes. "I don't know. I've never had a one-night stand. I don't want anything serious, and I guess I thought it would be nice to feel wanted for one night."

He ground his teeth. The idea of Kaylee with that guy made his stomach roil. He'd never been possessive of women. It was the reason he could walk away from them. Well, except for Kaylee. And maybe that was just the way it would always be. Which was why living in the same town —*working together*—just wasn't going to work. But he had too much on his plate right now to do anything about it. "Take it from me, you're not missing anything."

By the way her gaze softened, he was afraid she saw more than he wanted. "If hooking up with random people is so bad, why do you do it?"

"Boredom? Scratching an itch?"

It was more complicated than that. He'd not wanted a close relationship with a woman, and casual hookups kept him from thinking about why.

She pursed her lips. "You should call a doctor about that itch. It sounds nasty."

He snorted. "I'm as clean as spring rain."

"Why do I doubt that?" she said.

"My soul might be dark, but let's just say, I always sheathe up."

"You didn't always with me."

He stiffened. Not because they were talking about condoms. But because he wasn't prepared for her to bring up the past. And them. *Having sex.*

Images of them making love crashed over him. And the heat that had punched his chest earlier, after seeing her with some skeezy dude, rushed south, warming and inflaming. "We were careful... Most of the time." He gave her a cocky grin and her face paled.

"I gotta go," she blurted, and rushed past him, bumping into his arm as she did.

He caught up to her. "Hold up. I said I'd take you home. You're not driving in your condition."

"Fine."

Fine? No pushback?

Why did talking about their past sex life make her look like she wanted to puke?

Man, if Wes wasn't so confident in that department, Kaylee's reaction could have given him a complex. Good thing he knew better.

He guided her to his car and opened the passenger door, watching her closely. She staggered into the seat of his Range Rover, and he got the sense it wasn't all from alcohol.

He swept around the back of the vehicle, entered the driver's side, and turned the ignition.

This was what he'd wanted. To take her home. So why was his adrenaline rushing, his hands shaking? And not in the heated way they had earlier. Something was bothering Kaylee, and that put Wes on edge.

"Kaylee," he said as he pulled down the long drive of the Club Tahoe entrance. Her head was tipped against the seatback, her face pointed out the window. "Why did you get upset when I said we'd been careful? Because I sure as fuck was faithful to you, unlike that piece of..." He took a deep breath and let it out slowly. "What I meant to say is, I was a good boy back then. So why the sour expression?"

Her face scrunched up and she covered it with her hands, mumbling something that sounded like *baby*.

"What was that?" His senses went into hyper-alert. She wasn't acting normal. Not even for a drunken Kaylee.

She dropped her hands and stared down at them. "I lost our baby."

Her words had come out light, for all the weight they carried.

Wes's head swiveled to her and he swerved, nearly driving them into a ditch. "*Excuse me?*"

"Our baby." Her soft eyes were shining, face contorted in pain. Tears started streaming down the smooth skin of her cheeks. She looked away and huddled in the corner between the seat and door.

He glanced feverishly between her and the road. "What are you talking about?" But it was too late to get a coherent answer out of her.

She was crying harder than he'd ever seen her cry before, large convulsions racking her body as she rocked into herself.

Her head rolled against the seat, words flying from her lips in a drunken mumble-rant. "Can't talk about it. I thought I could. That if I came here, it would wipe away the guilt and sickness of it all. But it's still there." She pressed her fist to her stomach, moaning.

Holy fucking... Wes considered pulling over. This was

crazy. Kaylee was talking crazy. Should he take her to the hospital? Because something was seriously wrong.

But they were out in the middle of nowhere, and he was five minutes from her place.

By the time he reached her house, Kaylee was already passed out, her body jerking every few seconds from left-over crying hiccups.

Wes drew a heavy hand down his face and blinked at the front door. He stepped out of the car and strode across the driveway to the hide-a-key under a large fake rock her family hadn't moved since he dated Kaylee. He opened the door and returned the key to its hidden spot, then made his way back to the Rover.

Wes looked down at the small body huddled in the passenger side of his car. Kaylee's arms were wrapped loosely around her knees, and her soft, dark hair fell over her face. His chest compressed, his gaze softening for a second. Fuck. *Fuck*. She couldn't have meant what she'd said. This was drunk talk. This wasn't real.

He carefully opened the door and unlatched the seat-belt, easing her shoulders back. She mumbled, but didn't wake. He slid an arm beneath her knees and his other behind her back, lifting her out of the seat and cradling her to his chest.

He shut the car door with his foot and carried her into the house.

Scanning the place, he considered taking her upstairs and laying her on the bed, but he changed his mind. He needed to talk to her, and not in a bedroom.

Wes strode to the large sectional couch and laid her gently along the length. He found a throw blanket and draped it over her, then pulled off her heels and tucked the blanket around her feet.

Kaylee barely moved, but her chest was rising and falling in a smooth rhythm, the crying hiccups gone.

He sighed. He wasn't leaving her alone, that much was for sure. Not with her passed out. People died from alcohol poisoning. He didn't think she'd had enough to cause serious damage, but the words coming out of her mouth were insane, and anything was possible.

Wes went into the kitchen and grabbed a glass of water. He set it on an end table near her head, then kicked off his shoes and walked to the window that overlooked her parents' yard. They had a nice place nestled in the woods, yet close to town.

He rubbed his forehead and glanced at Kaylee's still body. God, he hoped she'd been talking gibberish about that baby stuff. Because if she hadn't, it would mean she'd lied to him all this time.

And that their past and why she'd left him was bigger than he ever imagined.

CHAPTER FIFTEEN

When she couldn't take the pounding in her head any longer, Kaylee opened her eyes. It was light out and she was...on the couch?

"Morning."

Her gaze snapped to the figure sitting near her feet. "Wes? What are you doing here?"

And then the pieces of last night slowly came together. The guy she'd considered going home with, just to put the past behind her. To feel desired when all she'd felt was a whole lot of nothing.

Wes had pulled her away from him. And then on the car ride home...

"Oh God." She sat up and wished she hadn't. The room spun and her stomach clenched.

"Water's right behind you," he said in that patient tone laced with anger.

Kaylee reached for the glass and sipped, cautious of her queasy stomach. She glanced at him over the rim. Wes's body was tense and he looked like he hadn't slept. As though he'd been sitting up all night, watching her. "Why did you stay?"

"You were drunk."

"Not that drunk."

His mouth crooked to the side. "You passed out, so yes, you were."

"Fine. I drank too much. It's been years since college. I'm a little out of practice."

Despite what she'd said to Wes last night, she wouldn't have gone home with the other man. Given the guy her number? Sure. She was single, and sitting around moping over her failed engagement wasn't the way to move on. She wasn't interested in anything serious, but dating someone nice didn't sound so bad. Though it would take her a while before she could fully trust again.

Wes sat forward, his large shoulders seemingly crowding her, when he was actually several feet away. "Do you remember what you said to me before you passed out?"

She'd returned to Lake Tahoe for her wedding, but also so she could tell Wes about the baby. To shed the guilt and shame and sadness, and finally explain what had happened all those years ago. And then she saw Wes for the first time —and he was still so angry.

She couldn't do it. Not while he hated her. Maybe it had been a mistake to come at all. But Wes had taken her home last night when he didn't need to. He'd shown up at her house, after she'd discovered Eddy's infidelity, just to make sure she was okay. Tension might still exist between them, but he cared, even if he didn't admit to it.

She'd almost convinced herself that he was better off not knowing about the past. That she could hold it inside and not release the pain on him. And then, in a single drunken moment, she'd shared all. The past that would never leave her—that ate at her from the inside out and had forever changed her life.

She'd blurted out the truth about the pregnancy, because deep down she'd selfishly needed him to know. Didn't want to be alone with it.

Kaylee rubbed her eyes and swung her legs over the side of the couch. "Can I brush my teeth and change before we get into this?"

He gestured lazily for her to go ahead, but every muscle in his body appeared taut.

Kaylee made her way up the stairs to her bedroom and brushed her teeth in the master bath, then changed, all the while trying to figure out how to tell Wes something she should have told him years ago. But it had been her body. She'd been the one irrevocably changed. So even if he'd had a right to know, she'd been too messed up and vulnerable to tell him.

She reached for a pill bottle, downed headache medicine, and scrubbed her face with a warm washcloth. She looked at herself in the mirror. From the outside, she appeared much like the girl Wes had fallen in love with in college, minus the long hair—but nothing was the same on the inside.

Kaylee made her way downstairs, and found Wes staring at the pine trees and mountains beyond from the tall dining room windows. It was her favorite place in the house too.

Padding quietly on bare feet, she entered the kitchen and made coffee, slowly ritualizing the process. Putting off the inevitable. Telling him the details about the pregnancy wasn't going to be easy, even after they'd spent time together.

Kaylee carried over two mugs and held one out to Wes.

He glanced up, blinking as though he'd been deep in thought, and accepted the coffee. "Thank you."

She sank onto the couch and wrapped her hands around the mug, soaking up as much strength as she could from the warmth. "About last night, and what I said. I'm sorry it came out like that. I'd had this perfect plan to share it with you when I first arrived. And then things unraveled. In the end, I thought it would be better to let the past stay where it was."

He shook his head forcefully. "That crazy talk was real? You had a...*a baby*? And you didn't tell me?"

Even after all these years, tears welled. "No. There's no baby."

Wes ran his fingers through his hair, making the beautiful, dark locks flop over his forehead. "I've been up all night trying to figure out what the hell you could have meant. You need to explain it from the beginning."

She closed her eyes. "Before your tour qualifying tournament senior year, I was sick. Do you remember?" He stared at her blankly. "No, of course you don't. You were too busy at the time." She set her mug on the coffee table and rubbed the tops of her thighs.

He looked around as though mentally searching. "You were...tired. More than usual."

"I was. I thought it was midterm stress. School draining me. I slept a lot. I wasn't interested in food... And then I started bleeding. You know I had an irregular cycle. I assumed it was just more of the same. But this bleeding came with intense pain."

His jaw tensed and he stared at her, waiting.

"I went to the school health clinic and they told me I was having a miscarriage." Wes dropped his head, and she took in a shaky breath, willing the quaver in her voice to stop. "I was three months pregnant."

"Fuck," he said. After a long moment, he looked up. "Why didn't you tell me?"

"*Tell you?* I didn't know I was pregnant. And when was I supposed to mention the miscarriage? While I was bleeding out—the same day you told me you couldn't focus on anything until after the tournament? Or when I had to have an emergency procedure to remove our baby that had died inside me?" She blinked back the tears. "No, Wes, I didn't tell you. I was in shock, barely holding on to my sanity."

He slumped back and covered his face with the palm of his hand. "I'm sorry."

A tear leaked over her cheek and she pressed her lips together. "You were unavailable—out of state for intensive training. I went home to recover, but I was still in pain. I saw my local doctor and he said"—she covered her face, the tears falling harder now—"he said there was so much scar tissue from the emergency procedure that was done, that I'd never get pregnant again."

She didn't see him move. Didn't hear him. But the next thing she knew, Wes was gathering her up into his strong arms and pulling her onto his lap. He rubbed her back and she cried against his shoulder, his hand shaking as it stroked the top of her head. "I was selfish. Young and stupid. I didn't know what I had," he said. "Didn't know what was important."

Not since she'd lost the baby, along with her fertility, had the weight she'd carried lifted. Until now, listening to Wes's soft words. This was what she'd needed. His support. His comfort. God, she had loved this man. A part of her still did.

She slid off his lap, her legs still covering his. He gripped her ankle, not letting her go. "I was angry at myself. At you. There's more to life than having children, but at the time, I wanted to marry you and have your babies." She sent him a self-mocking smile. "I felt like my life was over. I couldn't have stood seeing the same disappointment on your face. I sank into a deep depression and had to leave."

"I get that," he said softly. "And you had every right to take time for yourself. But why didn't you tell me once you felt better? Why did you dump me and never come back?"

She lifted her legs off his lap and eased them over the edge of the couch to the ground. "That's the thing. I thought *you* would leave *me*. I was in self-preservation mode. You'd been distant, and this was huge. I couldn't have stood you breaking up with me." Tears ran down her face, and she swiped them away with the back of her hand. "I was broken. Even if you had stayed, you'd never have looked at me the same."

His expression tightened. "Kaylee, I fucking *loved you*. Nothing you could have told me would have changed that."

The sincerity in his voice stole her breath. "I didn't know. I—I thought I loved you more. That I would tell you what had happened and you'd want a way out."

He stood abruptly, a slew of curses streaming from his mouth. "All this time." He shook his head. "I guess we'll never know what could have been."

He walked to the door.

"Wes." Kaylee scrambled to her feet, a horrible, sinking feeling settling in her stomach.

He opened the door and looked back, gaze unfocused. "I'll see you around."

The door closed and her legs gave out. She crumpled to the floor, silently crying.

She'd feared years ago that he would leave her if he knew the truth, but from what he said, she'd been wrong.

And if so, she'd lost more than she ever knew.

CHAPTER SIXTEEN

I t was dark out. Who knew how late? Wes was on his eighth bucket of balls at the driving range after a full day of tournament preparations and slipping in a round of shitty golf. He had his sponsor's exemption, but damn if he didn't want to prove he deserved to be out there.

Wes could sort of see where the balls were going. At least the trajectory. Didn't need to know exactly where they landed, as long as his form was perfect and the line and arc of the balls good. He'd been all over the map during this afternoon's round of golf, and that wouldn't do for the Tahoe Invitational. He couldn't fuck it up. No matter how messed up he was after the bombshell Kaylee had dropped on him this morning.

She'd had a miscarriage...and she hadn't told him. Worse, it had hurt her permanently. Physically, but also emotionally.

Sweat poured down his forehead, his lower back ached, and it felt like a spike was beating the shit out of his head. He gripped the club in his hand, his knuckles turning white. There was no way he could have predicted that avalanche of a secret. And he didn't know what to do about it. She'd stolen his ability to do anything, truth be told. Because she'd decided he didn't need to know about the baby. Not that he could blame her.

He *had* been self-absorbed. And not much had changed. Golf still ruled his world.

Wes positioned another ball and prepared to swing. Kaylee didn't believe in him. Not enough to tell him she'd lost their child. That lack of confidence...

"Wes."

His elbow dropped and he spun toward the voice.

Bran lifted his leg over the chain that blocked off the driving range. "What are you doing out here? Your phone dead or something? Levi's been trying to get a hold of you all afternoon."

Wes repositioned his club and swept it down and through the tips of the grass, sending the ball sailing into the dark universe. "I got his messages. Everything's on schedule."

Bran let out a harsh sigh. "Dude, you can't drop off the planet. Not now. Not when the club hinges on your part in this show."

The thing pounding inside Wes's head turned into a sledgehammer, his chest so tight he thought it would crack. He growled, swung his club in a wide arc, and launched it into the dark and onto the range. He turned to Bran, whose brow was raised. "I can't take this shit right now!" Wes clutched his head and paced back and forth. "*Not. Now.*"

You'd think Bran would give him some space, but no, his brother pulled off his ball cap and scratched his head, his dirty blond hair curling up at the ends. "Is it the tournament that's got you all riled up?"

"No." Wes's chin fell to his chest and he pinched the bridge of his nose.

"Then what?"

Wes looked up at the sky, blanketed in stars. "Kaylee. She... I fucked up, Bran. I'm a dick."

He heard his brother sigh. "You're not an intentional dick." Wes shot him a glare, which Bran ignored. "Kaylee knows that, or she wouldn't have been with you."

Wes swallowed. "I can't fix this. And it's my fault. She was pregnant. In college. I wasn't there for her and she lost the baby."

A burning sensation filled Wes's eyes, and he rubbed them. He wasn't crying. Losing a chance at the tour could make him cry, but not this thing that had happened a long time ago. No, his eyes were irritated from the grass, that was all.

His brother cursed. "Wes, I doubt you could have changed the outcome. It happens for no good reason to a lot of couples." There was something in Bran's tone...

Wes looked over, catching a dark expression he'd never seen on his brother's face before. "Did it happen to you?"

A beat passed, then Bran nodded. "In high school. It wasn't exactly the same thing, but I might have been a bigger dick than you back then, if you can imagine it."

Wes rocked back. How did he not know this? And coming from Bran? Never in his wildest dreams could Wes have predicted those words coming out of his nearly celibate brother. "Why did you never say anything?"

Bran started to pace. "Because I was an utter asshole and didn't handle it right? Because there was no one to talk to, except Levi, and he would have kicked my ass all over town if he'd known." He stopped pacing and stared out at the night sky. "She had an abortion."

Wes turned away. "What is wrong with us? Why are we all screw-ups?"

"We practically raised ourselves. That might have something to do with it. But Levi and Adam give me hope. Those two turned out okay."

Wes chuckled humorlessly. "Because they met Emily and Hayden, who kicked their asses until they got it together. Adam was no saint, and Levi was as self-involved as the rest of us, until he reconnected with Emily."

"True." A small smile crept over Bran's mouth, and then quickly disappeared. "Is Kaylee okay?"

"No. I'm pretty sure she's not. She said she was a mess after it happened. That she..." His voice caught. "That she can't have kids because of it."

"Jesus. I'm sorry."

A shred of vulnerability sliced through Wes's chest. "I don't know what to do. Don't know how to fix it."

"How can you fix what happened long ago? She didn't tell you about the baby until now, right?"

Wes sank onto the bench behind the range. "She said she didn't know she was pregnant until it was too late. I was focused on myself and pushed her away." He looked up. "She was three months pregnant, Bran, and I didn't know. Hadn't wanted to know, because my shit was more important. She was sick and I told myself she was fine. What kind of man does that? I loved her more than any woman, and I broke her heart." He stared down at his hands—large even for a man, refined like his father's. He'd not been there for Kaylee, just like his father hadn't been there for him. "Maybe it was my fault she lost the baby."

Bran rubbed his forehead. "That isn't how it works—not that I'm an expert. You can't beat yourself up over something you couldn't control."

Wes looked over. "Have you stopped beating yourself up? You've changed since high school, yet you barely glance at women."

Bran pulled his cap back on, his posture stiff. "This isn't about me. You have Kaylee back. If you want her."

Wes chuckled darkly. "You ever wonder why I never commit to women?"

"Because you're a player?"

He gave Bran a hard look. "Because I was so pissed at Kaylee for leaving me, I punished every woman that came after her. Wouldn't let them in, and I made damn sure they knew where they stood. I blamed Kaylee for everything, and it was never her fault. This whole time, it was me. I was the problem."

Bran rolled his eyes. "Okay, I'm only going to say this once, because I hate to inflate your ego. You're a good man, Wes. A gentleman. You never committed to women after Kaylee, but I've never seen you be unkind. If you hurt Kaylee, it was unintentional. And given that you're just finding out about this baby, she holds some blame in how things worked out."

"No she doesn't. She went through it alone. And then she found out that she couldn't have children. I'm responsible for that." Wes dropped his head into his hands, elbows on his thighs.

"Is there anything I can do?"

"Keep Levi at bay. Tell him I've got things under control." He lifted his head. "Every vendor I've spoken to has jumped through hoops to get me what I needed for this event. No one wants to be left out of something this lucrative."

Bran nodded. "Same here. I've got enough outdoor food vendors lined up to feed a small village... All right, I'll tell

Levi I've spoken to you. I don't suppose you want to tell him about Kaylee and the baby?"

"Fuck no. But I'll let Kaylee know I've told you. Sorry to unload. You caught me at the wrong time."

Bran slapped him on the shoulder. "Always here for you."

Wes and his brothers might have raised themselves and been independent, but they had each other's backs. They argued and fought, but were there when Wes needed them.

He stood and scanned the dark. *Dumbass*. Now he had to go find his favorite club, which he'd pitched into the night. "What time is it?"

"One. Go home and get some sleep. You sure you're going to be okay?"

No. "Yeah."

"I prefer Levi's couch if I'm going to crash at one of your places," Bran said, "but I'll sleep on yours if you need someone around."

"I'm fine. But—have you seen Kaylee today? Does she seem okay?"

"I saw her on the beach with her crew of kids. She's good with them."

Of course she was. She should have been a mother... Wes's throat locked up. "Okay then." He turned on his cell phone flashlight and headed into the dark for his club.

"Wes. Call me if you need anything. And consider talking to Kaylee. I'm going to take a wild guess and assume you haven't shared how torn up you are about the baby or what she went through."

Wes shot him a look over his shoulder. "What do you think?"

"Exactly. So maybe you should. It might make her feel better, and it might do you some good too."

"Nothing good can come from what I did to that girl."

"She's not a girl anymore," Bran called. "And she might appreciate a man humbling himself. Especially one who still loves her."

Wes nearly stumbled. The last place he wanted to delve was into his feelings for Kaylee. And how her leaving him had nothing to do with her not loving him and everything to do with Wes not being there for her.

If not for him, they might still be together. And that was something that stripped him raw. Because if he was honest with himself, he'd never gotten over Kaylee.

CHAPTER SEVENTEEN

Kaylee watched as the kids built sandcastles under Hunt's instruction. *Instructor* should be used loosely here, given Hunt was only marginally more mature than the children.

"No sand fights!" she called, shaking her head.

Hunt looked up from across the beach and raised his hands in confusion. But Kaylee had just seen him nail a kid in the back with a sand ball.

"It's no use."

Kaylee glanced behind her and saw Emily walking precariously across the beach in her heels, mouth twisted as she stared at Hunt.

Emily made it to Kaylee's side and squinted at the sandcastle melee. "He's like a larger version of them." She tipped her head to the side. "If you aren't looking directly, you might even mistake him for one. But he does make sure they're safe."

"That's true," Kaylee said, also staring at the "sandcastle building." Which was, essentially, about two hundred dollars of equipment, sand, and a whole lot of inexperienced builders digging and dumping sand everywhere. "He's fierce with his whistle when the kids get too close to the water. He's kind of paranoid about it, actually."

"You don't know the half of it," Emily said. "Hunt insisted on two lifeguards for the beach. It's overkill, but Levi relented because it makes the beach safer."

Kaylee glanced at the lifeguards on duty and snorted. "I'm going to assume Hunt chose them?"

Emily stared in utter seriousness. "Obviously."

The lifeguards Hunt hired were great at their job, even Kaylee could tell that much. And she wasn't a big swimmer. But Hunt chose *female* lifeguards, one blonde and one brunette. Both had slim figures and large breasts, and their faces and long hair were naturally beautiful. Neither of the girls could be a day over nineteen, and they were incredibly toned. Okay, they had perfect bodies.

Kaylee wasn't overweight, but she was a normal woman. She had dimples on the backs of her thighs. If these lifeguards had even a single dimple of cellulite on their flawless athletic figures, Kaylee would swallow a handful of sand. They were smooth-skinned and waxed to perfection.

Kaylee nudged Emily playfully. "You think he had them show up in their swimsuits before he hired them?"

Emily snorted. "Without a doubt. I mean, come on, Hunt Cade passing up the chance to see women nearly naked?"

They laughed, and it felt good. Ever since Kaylee told Wes about the miscarriage a few days ago, she felt like she'd lost something. She thought there wasn't anything left to lose. Not after she found herself starting her life over from scratch. Twice. But watching Wes walk out the door after she'd told him the truth, she realized she was wrong.

Whether she'd acknowledged it or not, she and Wes had

started to form a friendship again. And she hadn't realized how much that meant to her. Now she worried she'd severed anything that could have existed between them.

"He couldn't even get in trouble for sexual harassment," Emily said, still talking about Hunt. "He made a swim and rescue test as part of the job requirements. Everyone who applied—male or female—had to show up in their bathing suits."

Kaylee nodded sagely. "He is wily in his attempt to secure beautiful women for his inner sanctum."

Emily grinned, and then her eyes flashed to the side. She ducked a split second before a sand ball hit Kaylee in the back of the head, flinging her hair forward, along with sand into her face. "What the..."

Kaylee turned to find Hunt fist-bumping with Bella. "I saw that!" she shouted.

Hunt tossed something plastic over his shoulder. Likely the plastic snowball builder she'd bought for the kids.

Kaylee dusted off her face and shook out her hair.

"I'm sorry," Emily said, chuckling. "I saw it coming, and my first instinct was to duck and cover."

"Wise. I should have never bought those snowball things Hunt insisted he needed for this project. But he always comes up with fun things for the kids to do, which is why I put up with stuff like sand in my hair."

Emily bit her lip. "So things are going well? You're happy here?" She sounded anxious.

Despite Kaylee's reasons for coming to Lake Tahoe, and the fallout after those plans had imploded, she was happy she'd chosen to stay. No matter how things ended with Wes, this was the first time in years she felt like she could breathe. A part of that was finally telling Wes the truth, no matter the outcome. The other part was working at Club Tahoe.

The guys might fumble here and there as they tried to run the resort, but they'd brought something magical to the place, an energy that touched everyone who came here.

"I enjoy my job at Club Kids. It's not social services, but I still feel like I'm doing something special. No matter what's going on in these kids' lives, they can put that aside and come here, where it's safe to explore who they are and the world around them."

Bella peeled off from the group and worked her way over. She'd been around most of the summer, and Kaylee loved having her at Club Kids on a regular basis. Wes had taken her in and trained her at golf, but Bella seemed even more confident since Club Kids started.

Emily let out a breath. "I'm so glad to hear that you're happy with us." She beamed as she handed over a slip of paper. "This is an extra paycheck. I had finance draw it up instead of a direct deposit into your account. I wanted to give you the good news in person."

"Good news?" Kaylee accepted the slip of paper, watching Emily.

"The children's program has grown twofold since we started, and you've been instrumental in keeping it running efficiently and, more importantly, in helping the program flourish. The parents love you, the kids love you, and I love you. So we've given you a raise." She gave Kaylee a hug. "Never leave us."

Kaylee laughed. She might have even cried if she weren't in front of the children. Emily had no idea how much this program, and Levi and Emily's kindness, had given her since she moved to Lake Tahoe. "I don't plan to leave."

"Well, just in case you get other ideas, this raise should entice you to stay."

Kaylee finally looked at the check. "Wow. Emily, you didn't have to do that. But it does help knowing I can pay my bills if I need to move out of my parents' place. Thank you so much."

"The pleasure is all mine." Emily glanced up. "Looks like your kids need you. I'll leave you to your sand ball—I mean *sandcastle* project."

"Coward!" Kaylee called as Emily hurried away seconds before Bella reached her.

Bella flung her small, sandy arms around Kaylee's waist, giggling.

"What are you laughing about? I saw how you goaded Hunt with that sand ball. And since when is it okay to throw sand?" She pretended to spit out a granule, causing more giggles to erupt from Bella.

"It was Hunt's idea."

Kaylee narrowed her eyes in Hunt's direction. "I'm not surprised. In any case, no more throwing sand. We don't want the kids to get it in their eyes."

Bella peered past Kaylee and her arms loosened. "Wes!" she screamed, and ran off.

Wes was crossing the beach, one hand tucked in his golf khakis, a serious expression fixed on his face. His gaze flickered to Bella and softened as the little girl bounded near him.

Kaylee's stomach clenched and her heart raced. Telling Wes about the pregnancy—and her inability to have children because of it—hadn't gone the way she'd planned. She'd surprised him with the truth; she got that. Even if he'd comforted her for a moment, he'd done the one thing she'd always feared: walked out. And she hadn't heard from him since.

Bella leapt at Wes, and he gave her a quick squeeze. He

was a tall guy, well over six feet. And Bella was tiny. Wes always knelt when he spoke to Bella, like he was doing now.

He said something low in her ear and handed her an envelope. Bella nodded excitedly.

"How's Club Kids going?" he asked loud enough that Kaylee could hear.

"Great!" Bella said. "Hunt just nailed Kaylee in the head with a sand ball."

Wes's mouth twisted. "Is that so? Guess I need to teach Hunt a few lessons in sand balling after work." He looked at Kaylee. "You okay?"

"Nothing like chewing on sand grains for the rest of the day."

"I'll talk to Hunt."

She shook it off. "No, really, I'm fine. It was all in good fun. The kids love Hunt."

Wes stood and rested his hand on Bella's small shoulder. "That's because they recognize their own kind."

Kaylee smiled. "Emily and I were just discussing that."

The corner of Wes's mouth didn't so much as turn up as it softened. And that small gesture was a relief. She needed to know they were okay.

He looked down at Bella. "Well? What do you think?"

She held up the envelope he'd given her. "Look, Kaylee. Wes says I can go to the big golf tournament with my parents."

"That's wonderful, Bella. I'll be there too, and I'll make sure to look for you."

Bella ran back to the group, waving her hands and the envelope. She talked animatedly with the other children, likely sharing the news.

Kaylee was watching the kids, but she sensed Wes move to her side.

The skin along the side of her body sensitized—as though happily anticipating an accidental touch or brush of his arm.

She'd hoped that telling Wes about the pregnancy and why she'd left would create closure for them. But nothing was closed. And the tension between them hadn't entirely gone away.

Between her body anticipating Wes's touch and her anger with him for leaving her the other day, it was damn confusing—this mix of attraction and displeasure.

He nodded at Bella. "I'm giving a few star pupils passes to the tournament. I wanted Bella to be there, so she can see where she'll be someday."

"What if she decides to take up piano?"

He gave her a look. "Are you really going there again?"

She held back a smile. "It's possible."

A low growl rumbled from his chest. "No matter what she ends up doing...I support her," he said reluctantly, and she couldn't help laughing.

"You have a one-track mind, Wes Cade."

His face fell. She hadn't realized he was smiling with her until that moment. That the tension had eased for a second, until it was back.

His eyes flickered away. "I'm sorry, Kaylee. For being so focused on golf in college I forgot about everything else." He grabbed her hand and squeezed it, taking her by surprise. "Sorry I wasn't there for you."

She stared at their hands together, then back at his eyes, lighter in the sun. A royal blue and not the dark, cryptic navy swirls they were the other night.

She nodded, throat tight. This was the conversation she'd wanted to have with him. The mutual sharing of loss she'd not been able to express years ago. "I'm sorry I didn't say anything when it happened. The depression... It took hold and I couldn't see my way out of it. I lost direction."

He looked over her head toward the lake. "That's my fault. I didn't make it easy for you." His gaze dropped to hers. "But you can talk to me about anything from now on, okay?"

He was taking the blame, but it wasn't entirely his fault. She'd been an emotional wreck, and part of that was simply from a profound loss he couldn't have controlled.

She studied his handsome face, dark hair tumbling over his brow, those eyes so sincere. The way they used to be. Back when they'd first fallen in love...

Were they finally moving on? Finally putting the past behind them? He hadn't let go of her hand. And she really, really liked the way his hand felt wrapped around hers—warm and strong.

And then he did let go. "I better get back." He shifted his weight and hesitated. "One more thing. Adam and Hayden are going to invite you to the wedding. I wanted to give you a heads-up. Don't feel like you have to go or anything. If it's difficult or..."

She smiled. "It's fine. I'm not down on marriage. I should have ended my relationship with Eddy years ago, but hindsight is always clearer."

His gaze met hers and held. And damn those sensitized nerve endings. The cool, tingly sensation was all over the place this time—from the hair follicles on the top of her sandy head to the bottom of her exposed legs.

Her heart kicked up a notch, face warming, and she looked toward the kids.

Bella jumped on Hunt's back, and Kaylee smiled. That girl loved her some Cade men. Not that Kaylee could blame her. What wasn't to love? "There's always room for love and new dreams. I'll have that again someday."

"You will." He squeezed her arm and walked off.

Kaylee's stomach stopped swooning from that one touch, and she took a deep breath. Wes was Wes—he'd always make her head foggy. It didn't mean anything.

He'd had time to cool down and they were on good terms again, and that was all that mattered. After she'd emerged from her depression, making things right with him needed to happen. And now she finally had.

CHAPTER EIGHTEEN

Wes smirked as Levi tugged at the collar of the shirt beneath his tux.

"Hate these things," Levi grumbled.

Wes grabbed a glass of champagne from a passing waiter. "Really?" he said. "With all the times you've had to wear them lately, I thought you'd grown used to them."

Being the protector in the family wasn't the only reason Levi had originally chosen to become a firefighter. He was a jeans and T-shirt kind of guy. Being a firefighter suited his casual look. A nice flannel was about as flashy as Levi used to get. But all that changed once he became CEO of Club Tahoe.

Levi had stepped up his game in the clothing department. The results were hysterical. Oh, he looked as good as any of them in a suit, but Levi *hated* it. He bitched, he moaned—it was hilarious to watch.

Missing the sarcasm in Wes's tone, Levi said, "Still not used to them...but Emily likes me dressed up." A hint of bashfulness crossed Levi's face.

"So the velvet hammer is working her magic on you?"

"Shut it," Adam snapped from beside them. He pinched the bridge of his nose. "All of you." He included everyone in that statement, even Hunt and Bran, who'd remained silent thus far.

To say their bridegroom brother was a touch edgy was an understatement.

"Jesus, Adam," Bran said, voicing Wes's thoughts. "You're getting married today. What's with the anger?"

Adam's face turned a grayish hue.

Wes took a mental step back. Adam didn't look so good. "You okay there, buddy? Never thought you'd get cold feet marrying Hayden."

"Cold feet?" Adam said, clearly not getting the joke. "You idiot. I'm not getting cold feet over marrying Hayden. She's the best thing that's ever happened to me. If I could, I'd squirrel her away from this"—he glanced around the elaborately decorated ruby- and pearl-studded lobby—"*circus*."

Adam and Hayden were exchanging vows in the center of the island Wes's father had constructed when he'd first built the place. Guests would watch from the other side of the lazy river that circled it. "And away from you four. You're stressing me out."

Adam's face went from gray to purple. "If any of you so much as shoots someone else a glare, I swear, I'll... I'll take Hayden the hell out of here and never speak to you again." He tugged at the bottom of his jacket. Adam's tuxedo matched that of his brothers, with the exception of a red rose on his lapel instead of the ivory roses the rest of them wore. "Moving this wedding forward eight months has taken up all of our time, and I will *kill* you if you ruin this for Hayden."

"Fuck." Hunt's lip curled back. "Way to talk to your closest blood relatives on your wedding day. This isn't a very romantic mood you're setting."

Adam's hands clenched at his sides. "It *is* a fucking romantic day. So make sure it damn well stays that way, you cocksucker."

Levi carefully placed a hand on Adam's shoulder, who flinched in return. "Ease up there, Adam. No one's going to ruin your day." He glanced pointedly at each of them out of Adam's sight, as though to say, *Got that?* "Emily's in charge, remember? That means everything's going to be fine."

Adam let out a sigh. "Thank fuck or we'd all be fucked."

Hunt shook his head. "He's dropping F-bombs like they're going out of style. No, he's not nervous. Not at all."

Adam's head shot up and he stepped toward Hunt.

Adam wasn't his cool, polished self today. He'd turned into Levi when Levi was throwing down his alpha older brother shit. Or when Wes was in a foul mood—which was often.

Only Wes's foul moods had tempered since Kaylee dumped her fiancé. And even more so since he'd taken the time to consider their breakup, the miscarriage, and how he'd let her down.

Wes hadn't been happy with himself after Kaylee had told him the whole story about why she'd left. It was easy to blame her for not telling him sooner, but once he'd thought about it, he realized he'd been a big part of why she felt she couldn't talk to him, stubborn ass that he was. What he must have put her through... It made him want to tear down the walls of his one-room cabin. But at least now he knew what he'd done wrong and could fix it. Or try to.

Wes wasn't the same man he'd been. And he would

prove it to Kaylee. Because somehow, proving to her that he'd changed and matured was extremely important.

He'd apologized, and they were on good terms, but that wasn't enough. He wanted more with Kaylee.

This urge to win back his ex hadn't come to him in some great epiphany. It was a gradual realization since the first moment he'd set eyes on her inside the pro shop months ago. He'd told himself then that he'd get close to her and find out why she'd left him. That the knowledge would enable him to put the past behind him and get back his golf game.

What a load of bullshit. Wes had wanted to know why she left, because he'd never stopped loving her. Not that he'd admit that to a single living soul, but he wasn't such a caveman that he couldn't admit it to himself.

Okay, it had taken him years to admit it, but he'd gotten there eventually. Cavemen could evolve.

Levi swept in between Adam and Hunt, effectively blocking Adam from giving Hunt a shiner. "I see the brides-maids coming." Levi shoved Adam in their direction. "They're getting ready to walk down the aisle. We better take our places."

"Goddamn," Bran said when Levi and Adam were far enough away. "Remind me to never get married." He looked at Hunt. "We should ditch our plan for the reception. Adam is in a beast of a mood."

"Hell no," Hunt said. "Adam's just got cold feet. Once the vows are over, he'll be good as new. He's going to love what we arranged."

Wes sent him an incredulous look. "You and Levi started a fistfight in the middle of his engagement party. Can you blame the guy for thinking you might ruin this too?"

Hunt scrunched up his face. "That was forever ago. And what we have in store for the reception is going to blow his mind."

"Or have him killing us," Bran muttered.

Hunt stared out at the hundreds of guests finding positions across from the island. "Nope," he said confidently, "Hayden will love it. Thus, Adam will too."

And if she doesn't, Wes thought, *God save them from Adam's wrath.*

———

IT WAS the first wedding for any of his brothers—which was a scary thought for Wes. Most of them were in their late twenties, but still. Were they seriously nearing the age of matrimony? Would his balls start sagging now too? And where the hell was Kaylee in all this? Now that he'd figured out he wanted to prove to her he was worthy of a second chance, she was nowhere to be found. Typical.

Kaylee was supposed to attend the wedding, but Wes hadn't seen her since he'd arrived. Didn't help that Adam and Hayden had invited five hundred million people to this thing, or that a giant sagebrush blocked his view of the lobby from where he stood on the island, waiting for the wedding to begin.

Wes shifted his weight. Stupid sand was building up in his shoes. Whose idea was it to get married on the island, anyway?

The quartet near him struck a chord for the wedding march and everyone in the room grew silent. And then Hayden, dressed in a fitted gown that showed off her curves, started walking across the bridge to the island. She was on the arm of her father, her dirty blonde hair swept up, her warm brown gaze transfixed on Adam.

And Adam... *Dammit*, was Adam crying?

Yep, that was most definitely a tear he'd wiped from his cheek.

Okay, so it wasn't the manliest thing to admit, but whenever one of his stubborn brothers got choked up, it tended to make Wes choke up too. Not that Wes was crying. He just needed to take a deep breath.

And hold the air inside.

And...ahhh, *see Kaylee*.

Finally.

There she was, across the way in an emerald gown that draped to the floor, her dark, glossy hair tucked behind her ears, revealing sparkly earrings—all of it paling in comparison to how fucking gorgeous she was.

And now Wes needed to take a deep breath for different reasons. He'd forgotten how much her presence lit up his body like a firework.

The officiant went through the vows, Levi handed Adam the rings, and then, before Wes knew it, Adam was mauling his new wife like they were alone, not surrounded by hundreds of people. Okay, that was an exaggeration, but Jesus, get a room.

Adam turned toward the crowd, clinging to his bride's hand, and gave a shout of triumph.

Classy. Wes shook his head, a smile on his face. And this was his reserved brother.

The crowd erupted into cheers and hoots. When the chaos died down and the wedding party walked back over the bridge, Wes sought out Kaylee. But she wasn't where he'd last seen her.

Where the hell had she gone to now?

Wes congratulated the new couple, hugged a thousand grandmothers and aunts, and shook hands with another two thousand friends of the family. When he felt he'd paid his dues as a groomsman, he went in search of Kaylee, to make sure she was okay at a wedding all by herself.

At the wedding that should have been hers.

Jesus, maybe his boneheaded brothers could have thought about that before inviting her. She'd probably felt pressured into attending, since she worked here. Wes wanted her at the wedding, but not if it upset her.

He picked up his pace and started asking club workers if they'd seen her. But it wasn't until Adam and Hayden had danced their first dance as a married couple that Wes saw Kaylee.

The rest of the guests had sat down at the dining tables to watch the new couple, and Wes saw Kaylee toward the back of the room. She was talking animatedly to one of the other guests, likely charming him, her smile bright and genuine.

Wes's shoulders relaxed. He hadn't realized they were tense until he'd seen Kaylee smiling.

The man next to her leaned in. He was a handsome son of a bitch, with short, dark hair and a designer suit. Kaylee laughed at something he said. And Wes's initial instinct was to walk over and kick the guy out of the chair he'd scooted too close to Kaylee.

Wes was possessive of Kaylee, and only Kaylee. Always had been.

He looked away, attempting to chill the hell out. He even tried to chat with the bridesmaid to his right. But soon, he was staring over at Kaylee again—because he couldn't help himself.

Mr. Designer Suit was leaning on his elbow,

encroaching on Kaylee's personal space, as she seemed to be telling a story. The guy waved one of the servers over and had him pour Kaylee more wine.

Was he trying to liquor her up?

That's it. Wes had seen enough. The guy might have been acting out of politeness, but Wes didn't care.

He stood and walked over to Adam, who was ogling his new wife's breasts. "Shall we move this party forward?"

Adam looked up, startled. "What are you talking about? The wedding's been great, since you guys have been on your best behavior."

"Too true. We should change that." Wes nodded to Levi, who returned the nod and flagged the DJ.

Vivaldi's tranquil "Spring" halted and "Booty Wurk" kicked in.

Every one of Wes's brothers, with the exception of Adam, who gaped, eyes struck with terror, immediately stood and moved to the center of the room.

They spread out into a line facing Adam and Hayden. As soon as the chorus played, Wes and each of his brothers threw out their fists and hip-thrust to the beat.

It had been Hunt's idea to dance to a *Magic Mike* song at Adam's wedding. Who other than Hunt would come up with something like that? But once they'd talked about it over two—or seven beers—even Bran thought it a good idea.

They had no living parents. Only each other. The way Wes and his dumbass brothers showed their love might not be typical—fistfights, arguments, *Magic Mike*-choreographed dances—but no one expected the Cade sons to be conventional. It wasn't until their father's death that they'd even begun to clean up their acts and pull their lives together.

Hayden jumped to her feet and shimmied to the music.

She cupped her hands and hooted as they made another hip swivel—fucking Hunt and his dance choreography. Adam shook his head, but he was smiling too. How could he not? The entire room was cheering.

Catcalling was a perfectly acceptable form of praise to a man.

Hunt, the jackass, did a backflip, and then Wes and his brothers turned and thrust to the music for the guests seated behind them. For Kaylee. Whose jaw was unhinged.

Wes feigned grabbing a woman's hips and thrusting his dick toward her—yet another one of Hunt's choreographic masterpieces—but Wes was staring straight at Kaylee while he did it, envisioning her naked body against his.

The entire mental image put him at half-mast, but it was worth it for the look he received from her in return.

Kaylee's eyes fluttered and her gaze dropped to his waist. And then she did the most sexy, unaware thing ever. She licked her lips.

Jesus, yes. *I want that.*

Wes had convinced himself all these years that she was the villain. The one who'd ruined his life. But Kaylee had never been the bad guy. Wes had simply never gotten over her, and it was easier to blame her than to admit the truth.

Kaylee was still the same sweet girl he'd known, only she'd been through a tragedy and had grown stronger for it. She'd never let it change the person she was deep down. She was still kind and generous. Case in point, the way the children at Club Kids loved her.

Wes couldn't make up for his past mistakes overnight, but he could start. Who knew where things ended up from there? If only he didn't have this massive urge to go from zero to one hundred.

Watching Kaylee lick her lips and lift her sultry gaze to

his—she was sexy as fuck. And she was single. His lower brain thought, *Why wait?* Wes had a lot to make up for if she was ever to let him in again. And that was a big *if*. But none of that mattered at the moment. Suddenly his lower half seemed the smarter of the two brains, and it was in full control.

The music ended to thunderous applause and Adam and Hayden rushed the floor, dishing out hugs and patting backs as a new song came on.

"That was incredible!" Hayden said. "When did you have the time to practice? You've had the tournament to prepare for, you crazy men!"

Levi held tight to Emily, who'd run up to join them. "After hours. Hunt knew the moves. We just followed."

Adam shook his head. "Why am I not surprised Hunt was behind this?"

"You shouldn't be," Wes said, glancing to see if he could catch sight of Kaylee. But a woman he'd known for years, and unfortunately, had known intimately, came up and blocked his view of the woman he really wanted to talk to.

"That was amazing," she said. The blonde squeezed his biceps and slipped her arm around his back.

She was beautiful. And Wes felt abso-fucking-lutely nothing for her. And yet he'd slept with her, like he had with so many women. Killing time. Trying to not think about the past or all he'd lost. What he might never have again.

Wes squeezed out of her grasp. "Excuse me, I need to catch up with my brother."

"Smooth," Bran said after Wes made his way over.

Wes shrugged. "Not interested. No need to lead her on."

Wes wanted to find Kaylee and do a replay of the dance. With her. Naked in his arms. No one else.

Bran's eyes widened. "Incoming."

For a second, Wes thought the blonde had followed him. But when he looked, a redhead in a black gown was headed for Bran, and she looked like she meant business. "I think she likes you."

"She's been staring at me all night," Bran grumbled.

"Pretty."

Bran shot him a hard look. "Yeah, well, I'm not interested."

"In pretty?"

Bran shook his head and peered around. "I gotta go." He darted off before the redhead could make it over.

She frowned and shifted her direction, walking away, her confidence visibly flagging.

Meanwhile, Bran had gone up to one of the new waitresses they'd hired and was talking to her shyly. The poor girl appeared thunderstruck.

Bran was a handsome bastard. Could get any woman he wanted. And that was attraction for you, because the waitress he'd walked up to was on the plain side. Not that looks were all that mattered.

Wes had slept with plenty of beautiful women, and the one he couldn't stop thinking about could be dressed in a potato sack with her hair standing on end, and he'd want her. Because Kaylee's beauty wasn't only physical.

Attraction was more than looks. It was that thing that set your body buzzing despite appearances or logic. Call it pheromones, or whatever, but that shit was powerful. And Kaylee's pheromones had Wes's lower brain firing on all cylinders.

He understood now why Kaylee had ended their relationship in college. He thought it would help his golf game to know the facts, but it also brought him closer to the woman he'd loved.

And it was time to do something about it.

CHAPTER NINETEEN

"Care to dance?" Wes grabbed Kaylee's hand and practically lifted her out of her seat and onto the dance floor.

What was he up to?

Kaylee glanced back and gave the nice man she'd been talking to an apologetic smile. "Do I have a choice?" she said as she stumbled behind Wes.

He pulled her close and wrapped his strong arms around her waist, rocking to a slow song from the eighties. "No."

"Good to know." She breathed in. God, he smelled good. Why did her ex have to smell so incredible?

She'd always liked dancing with Wes. And it was a good thing, or he'd have a sore shin right now for hauling her away like that.

She cocked her head. "Those were some impressive moves you performed out there. Didn't know your hips could gyrate like that."

"There's a lot you don't know about me. I'm a changed man."

She held back a smile. "With limber hips as proof."

He looked up, as though considering. "Proof of my extracurricular talents, yes. But to find out how the rest of me has changed…" His dark blue gaze skimmed down her body. "We'll have to spend more time together."

Her eyes narrowed and her heart hammered in her chest. "I thought we did that at the driving range. You know, all those grueling hours of practice you put me through?"

He chuckled. "Nah, that was just me laughing while Bella tried to teach you how to swing a golf club."

"Hey!" She swatted his shoulder where her hands rested. And tried not to feel him up.

Wes had always been sexy and handsome, but now he was filled out and rugged, his five o'clock shadow already showing, though he must have shaved before the wedding. Her single-lady hormones liked the older Wes a little too much for Kaylee's comfort.

"Bella's a golf prodigy," she said. "And it's not polite to point out that a five-year-old is better than me."

He smirked. "My apologies. But I would like to spend more time with you—outside of the driving range."

Her smile faded and she studied his face. He was serious? "Why? We've only recently cleared the air over the past, and you didn't seem pleased to have me at your brothers' beer night."

His face hardened. "That was because you were flirting with another man."

"You were *jealous*?"

He tightened his arms around her. "Jealous of the guy drooling all over you tonight during dinner too."

She chuckled. "No need to be. I just met Ted. I barely know him."

"He wants you."

She shook her head. She might be attracted to her ex, but that didn't mean it was a good idea to go there. "Why would it matter?"

He seemed to catalog her features, his gaze dropping from her eyes to her nose to her lips... "Do you need me to spell it out?"

"Yes." Wes was...well, Wes. The man was handsome as hell, confident, and she wasn't kidding about the hip-gyrating thing. It had been erotic and made her think of *other stuff*. But no way would she give in. Her mouth firmed and her voice turned icy. "You've been hot and cold since I came into town. What is it you want?"

He grabbed her bottom and pulled her up, searing her lips with a quick, hot kiss. "Let's try again, Kaylee," he said low, hovering above her mouth.

Wes lowered her to the dance floor but kept her pressed against his chest and thighs.

Her breaths came out choppy. She tried to respond—to unleash some fury on his ass—but his hands on her bottom were ruining her concentration.

She eased back a few precious inches. "Are you insane?"

His gaze fell to her lips, like he might take her mouth again. "Not in the least."

She couldn't help it: she laughed. This was absurd.

"Why are you laughing?" he said. "Do you find it funny that I'm attracted to you?"

Her smile fell and a wash of exhaustion came over her. "*Tragic*—I find it tragic we're eternally attracted to each other. That's just cruel on the universe's part."

He dipped his head and breathed in beneath her ear. "Not tragic. Maybe it's destiny."

She jerked back. "Holy shit. That was the corniest line that's ever left your lips."

He shrugged one shoulder. "Can I help it if poetry spouts from my mouth when you're near?"

She laughed. "I'm not sure I'd call that poetry."

He frowned and squeezed her bottom tighter. Fortunately, the dance floor was crowded, or they'd be putting on a show right now.

"Wow. Okay. You really want this?" She watched him leerily, though she was silently soaking up the heat of his body, *because Wes.*

Kaylee had always been attracted to this man. Nothing had changed there. It was everything else that had shifted.

"We're older, more mature," he said as though reading her thoughts.

"Exactly, which means we have to be able to do better than rebounds and repeats."

"I'm not the one rebounding," he said, and led her to the side of the dance floor as a fast song came on. "And there was nothing wrong the first time we dated. Just bad timing and miscommunication."

She pulled on his hand to get him to stop and look at her. "There was so much wrong the first time. It tore my world apart."

He squeezed her hand. "My biggest regret is what you went through and that I wasn't there for you. But not everything between us was wrong. We can't help what happened. That part was a tragedy, but the rest..." He stared into her eyes. "I've never felt for anyone what I feel for you."

Feel. He said *feel*—as in present tense.

Wes slid his hand to her lower back and walked them toward the ballroom exit. The only reason he got away with it was because she was still reeling over his declaration of "feelings."

"That's not enough," she finally said, attempting to clear her head. One of them had to think straight, because she could easily see herself falling for Wes again. And that was frightening.

Falling for Wes nearly killed her the first time.

"Where are you taking me, anyway?" She glanced back.

He gave her a wicked grin. "Out."

"But the wedding—"

"Is over. There's only dancing left."

"Exactly. Dancing. The reception? Won't your brother be angry?"

He shrugged lazily. "Probably. But only until he leaves with Hayden. For some reason, this wedding has him stressed out."

"Weddings can do that."

He looked down at her, concern in his eyes. "Are you sad? That today should have been your day?"

She shook her head slowly. "No. I'm relieved. Discovering Eddy had cheated saved me from a divorce. His infidelity didn't change what was already wrong. It was never right between us; I know that now."

Wes nodded and walked on, out the back doors and past the lazy river. They turned into a semi-hidden nook with two lounge chairs behind the fire pit island. The nook had a pristine view of the lake and a part of the South Lake Tahoe lights.

Obviously, Wes knew every inch of the club. Including supercool hidden spots with great views. She wondered if he took many women here.

He gestured for her to have a seat on one of the lounge chairs. "Would you like anything to drink? Champagne?"

She held up her hand. "No. Thank you. I'm tempering my alcohol consumption after the Fireside Lounge with you and your brothers. Clearly, I'm a lightweight these days."

He unbuttoned his tuxedo jacket and straddled the lounge chair next to her, easing down with his arms folded behind his head. "I guess that night got us to this point. What you said might have slipped out eventually, but I'm glad it came out sooner rather than later. I would have always wanted to know."

"I should have told you years ago."

He looked at the view. "Things work out the way they're meant to. We're here now. That's all that matters."

She felt his stare land on her again. The heat of it. The weight. "Speaking of here and now," he said, "why don't you come closer?"

She tilted her chin down. "You're bad. I can't believe you kissed me in front of everyone."

"Come on, Kaylee. That kiss had been brewing for weeks. It was inevitable."

It had been, much as she was loath to admit it. And it *was* cold out. The season had turned quickly from summer to fall, the chilly air nipping at her skin.

Who cared what they did? Especially now that there were no more secrets. They were both single... "Fine. But keep your hands to yourself."

"I am a *gentleman*. I would never touch a lady. Unless she asked me to."

Kaylee heard the humor in his tone. Saw the twitch of his lips. She rolled her eyes but scooted onto his lounge anyway.

Of course he didn't give her room, which meant she was smashed up against him, practically sitting on his lap. "You can put your arms around me. It *is* cold out. And it'll prevent me from falling off this thing, since you've given me half a cheek's worth of space." She shot him a disgruntled look over her shoulder.

It was all for show, though, because she liked being right up next to Wes. He said he'd never felt for anyone what he felt for her. Well, she'd never loved anyone the way she'd loved him.

Wes sat up and took off his jacket, then draped it over them. He slid his arms around her waist, tucking her head beneath his chin.

His hand made a lazy pass up and down her arm. "Better?"

Better? It felt amazing. Like there was nowhere else she should have been all this time except in Wes's arms. But that couldn't be right. This wasn't real. The past was real—visceral.

She spun around until she was facing him, her chest pressed to his. "Why was golf more important than me?"

The kiss, them hanging out—it wasn't going anywhere, even if she was attracted to Wes. She didn't know why she felt the need to dredge up history, but she did.

Fine. She was considering seeing him again as more than friends, since he'd put his lips and hands on her, igniting all sorts of naughty thoughts. And if she was considering naughtiness, she needed to know what had gone on inside that stubborn man brain of his when they'd dated.

Wes adjusted his arms with the new position, but kept them wrapped around her. She sensed him shake his head above hers. "Golf was never more important. You were..."

She lifted her chin so she could see part of his face. "I was what?"

He leaned back and looked down. "Everything."

CHAPTER TWENTY

Wes lifted Kaylee's chin and kissed her lips lightly. When she didn't object, he slid his hand to her lower back and pulled her closer, dropping his mouth to hers again and parting her lips.

His heart thundered in his chest, his body heating. He might combust just from the glide of her tongue against his. And then she pulled away.

"What do you mean I was everything? Clearly I wasn't, or I would have never broken up with you."

He scrubbed his face with his hand. "In my head you were everything. I just...didn't know what I was doing. You know I didn't grow up with a mother. And my father wasn't around much. I learned about affection from my brothers." He smirked. "Think about that. It's like the blind leading the blind. The only thing we had going for us was that we were loyal. But there was competitiveness. A need to win and prove one's worth—or that could have only been me."

He looked intensely into her eyes. "Success in golf was what I thought I needed to deserve you. It wasn't until you came back into my life that I realized I'd only needed you."

Her eyes widened and she stared at him. "Damn you," she said. And then she pulled his head down and attacked his mouth with her tongue and her lips and her teeth.

He tilted her chin with his thumb and forefinger, getting just the right angle to love on Kaylee's beautiful, full mouth. To taste and worship her the way he'd been secretly fantasizing about these last few weeks.

He'd told himself that the reason she was in his dreams at night was because she was the woman he'd spent the most time with. That he checked her out when she wasn't looking, because she was a beautiful woman.

It was all a load of crap.

He wanted her.

He'd meant what he said. Golf had never been more important than Kaylee. But what was he without his sport? He'd never been good at anything besides golf. And he thought he wasn't enough for her without it. But fuck that. If she was willing to stick around, he was going to do everything he could to make her happy.

He'd won the jackpot when this beautiful girl had shown up at a college party and turned out to be the perfect woman for him. He'd thought all he needed was to build a life for them. But somewhere along the way, he'd lost track of what *she* needed. And then he'd lost her entirely.

Now Kaylee was back. And he wasn't letting her go so easily.

She wrapped her arms around his neck, and he took the opportunity to glide his hand down her waist and over her hip. He gathered the fabric of her dress and ran his fingers over her silky leg. And then he eased it over his own, bringing her closer.

Kaylee moaned, and his eyes nearly rolled into the back

of his head at the feel of her heat pressed against his erection.

His dick was in its happy place, so close to Kaylee and yet not close enough. But that was fine. Wes could deal with this form of punishment. It was the pain he'd experienced after she'd left him that he didn't want to go through again.

He kissed her neck and the top of her breasts. "Do you want to take this somewhere more private?" Pain or no pain, Wes had ideas. Slippery, naked ideas. And why the hell not? This was *his* girl—the only one he'd ever claimed.

He tugged her bra down and darted out a tongue to her nipple.

She pulled at his hair, rubbing against him. "Huh?"

"Too public here. Anyone could walk by."

"What do you suggest?" Her voice came out breathy and a little high—just like it used to when she was turned on.

He grew harder.

He kissed her long and deep. "That a yes?"

She hesitated, giving him just enough of a pause to make him worry she might say no. "Yes."

He grinned and pulled her up.

"Wes," Kaylee said as she tried to keep up. He might have been walking fast. "Where are we going?" She glanced back in the direction of the lounge chairs he'd had placed for his private use.

Most people didn't know about his secret spot. The chairs were tucked away, and he went there when he needed time to himself. Occasionally, one of his brothers joined him. It was private, but not nearly private enough for what he had in mind.

"I could carry you if your feet hurt," he said. "Do you want to hop on my back?"

"Or, here's an idea," she said sarcastically, "you could slow your pace."

Was it his fault he was in a hurry? This was going down, and there was no way he'd waste the opportunity. "Can't. I want to get right back to where we were." He looked back and grinned. "Ever gotten naked on a golf course?"

"You are very presumptuous."

"Wishful. Now, answer the question."

"No. You know I haven't. Who would I have been naughty with on a golf course, except you?"

"True." He squeezed her hand. "Let's remedy that."

She tugged on his arm. "I don't want to go to your favorite hookup spot, Wes Cade."

He placed his other hand on her soft, small bottom and hurried her along. "I've never hooked up there before."

"Never?" He felt her stare. "Not once?"

"Nope. It'll be my first time too. And that makes sense."

She tucked the arm he wasn't holding around her waist. The temperature was dropping quickly. Even Wes felt the cold. He'd given her his jacket, but she was wearing a thin dress. "How so?"

"Because I'll be making love for the first time on a golf course—with the only woman I've ever loved."

Kaylee stopped and let out a heavy sigh, but she was squeezing his hand and staring at his mouth. "Super presumptuous."

"Hopeful, Kaylee. Hopeful."

"I never could resist you. And now you're bringing out the big guns with that sweet talk."

He cupped her face. "I want to try... If you'll give me another chance?"

She blinked for several seconds, studying him. "Let's start with sex and go from there."

He grinned and squeezed her to his side, lifting her off the ground. "My favorite place to begin."

———

KAYLEE LET OUT A SQUEAK. "Wes! You just broke a rib."

"Sorry." He set her down gently. "Wait here, okay?"

Kaylee stared, dumbfounded, as Wes jogged toward the pro shop.

He wouldn't, would he? "Wes, if you even *think* about grabbing your clubs to hit a few balls, I swear to God, you will find yourself without your favorite pair!"

Wes froze with his hand on the door handle. "Crap, Kaylee, don't put that image in my head when we're about to get busy."

But he was smiling as he swept inside the store. He returned a few seconds later with what looked like cloth inside clear plastic.

Wes tucked it under his arm and grabbed her hand. "Blankets." He held up a box of condoms. "And other essentials." He waggled his eyebrows.

Was she really doing this? Having sex with her ex? "You sell condoms in the pro shop?"

"Men play golf, Kaylee. Sometimes they need a few items before they leave for the day."

"I'm a woman, and I play golf."

"Fine, carrying condoms was my idea." He grinned devilishly. "It's convenient."

She rolled her eyes.

"Did you really believe I'd grab my clubs after everything we've been through?" He sounded sincerely hurt.

She glanced at him out of the corner of her eye. "You've done it before."

He stopped and gently turned her to face him. "And I learned my lesson. There is nothing—*nothing*—I'd rather be doing right now...than you." He grinned lewdly.

Kaylee smacked Wes in the chest. "That is not romantic!" she said, but she was laughing, because he was kissing her neck and tickling her sides.

"You said you only want sex." He picked her up and threw her over his shoulder. "I'm your man."

She loved the playful side of Wes. She wasn't ready for anything serious. Not after her failed engagement. But this was nice.

Technically, she had no business getting into a relationship at all. But she was ridiculously attracted to Wes, and he wasn't declaring love or anything. He seemed perfectly happy with casual. And Kaylee was okay with that, because she felt safe with Wes.

Stomach smashed against his shoulder, she looked down at the box in his hand. "You know, you won't need those."

He snorted. "Trying to trap me?"

"You are such an ass! I can't get pregnant, remember? Only you could make my heartache a joke." Her words were serious, but not her tone. Guys weren't the sharpest when it came to feminine things, and Wes was probably just being careful.

He squeezed her legs. "Not a joke." He let her body slip down his chest, but not seductively. He stopped her glide downward once they were at eye level. "I'm so fucking sorry, Kaylee. Sorry that I'm the reason you can't have kids."

She rubbed her thumb along his full bottom lip. "It wasn't your fault. You had no control over what happened. But you really don't need those condoms. Unless you've been a dirty boy. Jesus, when was the last time you were checked?"

He tossed the box of condoms over his shoulder and hiked her back up. "Told you, I'm as clean as spring rain. Got checked out a few weeks ago. Besides, I haven't had sex without a condom since we were together. Holy fuck, I can't wait to get inside you."

He started running—*running*.

"Slow down!" she said as she bounced on his shoulder. "Do you have any idea how uncomfortable this is?"

"Can't slow. Need to get you somewhere private and divest you of that dress before you change your mind."

"This isn't a done deal! Have you no shame?"

"None." He slid her down his body, and this time his mouth was turned up in a cocky grin as she glided over all the bumps and ridges of his hard, muscled frame.

When her toes hit the ground, he leaned down and kissed her gently, but her head was spinning and her body tingled in strategic places. He totally did that on purpose to drive her crazy.

Wes stood there for a moment, not making a move, simply studying her face and looking into her eyes. "Kaylee." He shook his head. "I can't believe you're back."

Too much—this wasn't just sex for Wes, and it wasn't for her either, but she wanted it to be for now. It was the only way she could let go and enjoy being with him.

She cupped his erection and wrapped her hand around his neck, pulling him down so she could bite his lip. "Take off your pants," she murmured.

Wes growled and kicked off his shoes. He dropped his pants while trying to kiss her.

She laughed as he stood there in his boxer briefs and white tux shirt. "Holy shit, you really want this."

He tore off his bow tie and whipped his shirt over his head until he was in nothing but the boxer briefs—and suddenly she wasn't laughing anymore.

Wes was filled out and sexy as hell, looking at her like he wanted to lick every inch of her body.

Kaylee's breaths grew uneven.

He wrapped his arm around her and pulled her closer, kissing the top of her shoulder as he unzipped the back of her dress, smooth as could be. "You're so beautiful." He lifted his head. "No one is more beautiful than you."

She ran her hands down his warm chest. *Sex.* This was only sex. With a man she genuinely loved, even if that love was tangled with the past. She'd take his body and whatever he was willing to give, because she needed him. God, she'd needed him for so long.

Wes slid her dress down her legs, then tore open the plastic bag and shook out what appeared to be an outdoor blanket. He laid it on the green of the eighteenth golf hole, which was surprisingly secluded at night, then reached for her hand and tugged her until she fell onto his chest.

He eased them to the ground and held her like that, chest to chest, trailing his fingers gently up and down her back and over her ass. He let out a rough sigh. "You feel incredible."

"You're just saying that because you want to have sex without a condom."

He stilled. "*Fuck.* You had to remind me. I'm trying to take things slow."

His erection jerked against her belly and she reached for it, stroking him. "Has this gotten bigger since we dated? You're not taking supplements, are you?"

He flicked off her bra and loomed over her, the heat from him keeping her surprisingly warm despite the cool air. "Quit joking around. I'm serious about my need to be inside you. And no, my dick hasn't grown, it's always been massive."

She rolled her eyes as she watched him studiously slide her nude panties off and kiss her just above the juncture of her legs. "No arrogance there," she said breathily, trying for a light tone, but distracted by the man devouring her with his eyes.

Wes kissed a path up the side of her leg, his hand running up the other. "Your skin smells exactly the same— like coconut and honey." His dark blue gaze lifted to hers. "Makes me want to lick you."

"Filthy."

Another devilish grin flashed her way. "You have no idea." And then he spread her legs and licked her core, his fingers caressing just outside of where his tongue was working its magic.

Oh God. "You seem to have...acquired new skills."

A grunt sounded from down below, and then he turned his head, and his tongue did some sort of side-lapping thing that had her making embarrassing sounds.

"*Shhh*, Kaylee," he said quietly, seductively, his breaths passing over her tender flesh. "We don't want anyone to find us here." And then his head dipped again and he was back to the side tongue thing, sending her into immediate mini-orgasms that shot flashes of light through her head and had her core contracting, building up to something massive.

She grabbed the sides of his head as soon as her own stopped going off like firecrackers, and dragged him up by the ears. "Inside me. Now."

"You sure you want this?"

God, she didn't know what he meant. For him to be

inside her? Yes, for sure. She hoped he wasn't referring to anything more. "Yes."

Wes pulled off his boxer briefs, braced his corded arms near her head, and eased inside her.

His jaw tightened and he let out a slow breath. "Okay, we're going to take this slow so that I don't embarrass myself. I forgot how good you feel." His head dropped, his hot breaths sawing in and out near her ear.

Deciding to ignore his request, because she was kind of hot and bothered, Kaylee rocked her hips, and he groaned.

He must have gotten things under control, because he started rolling into her, his hips making small, tight circles that ramped her up from mini-orgasms to bringing on the big one.

"Don't shift or move," she ordered. "Just keep doing that. Feels so good."

And like the good soldier he was, Wes kept the same pace, same position—until she came with such force that her head slammed into the blanket-covered ground.

Wes cupped the back of her head and shifted until he was plunging into her deeply, stroking the spot he'd just worked over.

His movements were no longer smooth, and with one last thrust, he filled her, moaning out his own orgasm. His body eased slowly in and out of her a few extra strokes, light, jerking movements racking him.

He kissed her cheek, her mouth, then dropped his head to the side of hers, his breaths heavy, as though he'd just sprinted a mile. "Are you sure you can't get pregnant? Because I think I just impregnated you."

She smiled. "That's not funny." But it was, because this was Wes and he meant no harm.

Kaylee's legs were spread wide, her first love filling her

and caressing her temple with his thumb. She didn't even think he noticed he was doing it.

He shifted one hand beneath her ass, wrapped his other behind her back, and rolled her on top of him while he was still deep inside her. "You should know, I'm not leaving your body. It's my happy place."

"The wedding party might have a problem with that if they find us like this."

"Fuck them. I have you, and I'm not letting you go this time."

CHAPTER TWENTY-ONE

Kaylee lifted her head off Wes's chest. "You're not letting me go, eh?"

"Nope." He snuggled her closer, pressing her head back down. "Consider yourself under lock and key."

"Wow. You've gotten possessive since we dated." But she loved that he appreciated her and wanted her near. Eddy had always put his friends first.

Then she remembered how Wes had made golf his first priority.

"I've always been possessive," he continued, unaware of the thoughts running through her mind. "Made one stupid mistake and got distracted by golf, and you slipped by me. Not making that mistake twice."

She lifted up again and stared down at him, because this needed to be said, even if she appreciated his words. "I just got out of an engagement. I'm glad you've matured since we dated. But this"—she waved haphazardly around them—"is as far as things go."

His grin appeared forced. "Sure. But I might try to attack you later."

She let out the breath she'd been holding and flopped back onto his chest. "Oh, that's fine. Attack away. As long as it's just sex."

Kaylee had always been a relationship person. Having casual sex had never occurred to her until recently. It probably had something to do with her partner. Wes wasn't a stranger. And she believed him when he'd said he'd not meant to hurt her all those years ago. "Casual I can do. Especially now that you've become the Olympian of oral sex."

"Olympian." She heard the smile in his tone. "Nice. But Kaylee?" He waited until she tilted her chin up. "That was only a taste of what's to come."

Her stomach clenched. That was all it took—Wes's deep, sexy voice making promises of orgasms in her future, and she turned into a pile of mush.

He squeezed her ass. "Come on. Let's go back and get some food. I'm starved."

Food? Yes, food. That was a good distraction. Because she couldn't really be thinking about round two so soon. Okay, she totally, totally was.

He reached for her dress as she lifted off him, and he handed it to her.

Kaylee watched Wes pull back on his tux. She loved the way he moved. The confidence in every action. He didn't care about wrinkles or mussed-up hair. He ran his fingers through it and called it good, tucking his hand into the pocket of his tux pants while he watched her with a sultry smile. He was masculine, driven, yet such a giver. Wow, was his tongue ever a giver. And his hands...

Kaylee bent to put on her shoes—and to hide her face so he didn't see the flush that had risen to her cheeks. Wes was arrogant. No need to inflate his head further. God knew where they'd be then.

She straightened and smoothed out her dress. "I'm leaving it up to you to explain to Adam where we've been."

He grabbed her hand and kissed her knuckles. "No worries. I've got it covered."

———

AS SOON AS Wes and Kaylee returned to the reception, Kaylee headed for the bathroom.

Wes caught a glimpse of Adam saying something to Hayden, and then his brother was crossing the room with purpose. He grabbed Wes by the arm and dragged him into the corner. Not that Wes couldn't have broken his brother's grip. They were the most equal in height and weight. Physical fights between him and Adam were always a toss-up. "Where in the hell did you go? You've been gone the entire reception!"

"Not the entire reception. Only the dancing portion."

Adam frowned, and it sounded like he was grinding his teeth.

"Adam," Wes said, "you might need medication if this is what married life does to you. What gives? You're as wound up as a Pamplona bull."

Adam huffed out a sigh and glanced away. "Hayden put sex on hold until after the wedding. Wanted our wedding night to be special."

Wes raised an eyebrow. "How long has it been?"

"Four weeks."

"Jesus Christ." Wes looked around dramatically for one of his other brothers. "We should get you to the hospital."

"Don't be an idiot," Adam said. "I was never like you and Hunt. Didn't need a different woman every night."

"Oh really? And how's your sex drive now that you have Hayden in your life?"

Adam swallowed. "I'll admit, I'm a little edgy having her around and not *having* her."

"So what the hell are you still doing here? Go claim your woman."

Adam's cheek pulled back in the beginnings of a smile and then he frowned. "Can't." He ran a hand over his mouth. "Promised Hayden we could have this 'after the reception' pizza and cocktails thing. Our wedding was so large, she wanted to do something special for our close friends."

"I won't say anything if you two sneak off. Just do it, man, before you implode."

"I wouldn't be feeling the need to implode if you jack-asses weren't being such jackasses."

"Yes you would."

"Yes I would." He looked pleadingly at Wes. "How do I get her out of here without upsetting her?"

Wes put his hand on his brother's shoulder and leaned in. "Here's what you do..."

Moments later, Kaylee returned. "Have you seen Hayden?" She peered around. "I wanted to congratulate her, but I can't find her anywhere."

"Yeah, that's because I helped Adam slip her out," Wes said.

She stared at him. "You did?"

He shrugged. "Adam wanted to start the honeymoon. And I'm romantic like that."

She crossed her arms. "And this had nothing to do with Adam being upset because we left?"

"*Unreasonably* upset. He wouldn't have been wound up so tight if Hayden hadn't put the kibosh on sexy time until their wedding night."

Kaylee's face softened. "*Awww*, that's sweet. She wanted it to be romantic."

He stared at her in horror. "Don't get any ideas."

"Wes, you won't be at my wedding, so don't worry about what I will or will not be doing."

Yes I will, he thought.

Wes swallowed. That was nuts. He wanted to date Kaylee again, nothing more. He might be ready for something solid between them—more so than she was—but he wasn't ready to tie the knot.

"How did you help Adam get her to leave early, anyway?"

"Told him to tell her he had a gift waiting in the presidential suite that couldn't wait."

"And does he?"

Wes gestured in the vicinity of his cock.

She squinted. "Are you kidding me? Hayden will be pissed once she finds out he made it up just to get her naked."

"Probably. But only until my brother makes her happy in bed."

"If they make it to the bed before *she kills him*." She shook her head. "You Cades are really something, you know that?"

"You say that like it's a bad thing." He wrapped his arm around her lower back. "Let's get out of here. We'll catch up with my brothers later. Not like we don't see them every day, or anything." He glanced down pointedly. "Besides, I'm ready for round two."

"Ha!"

He leaned in until his mouth was millimeters from her ear. "My tongue is feeling restless."

He heard her swallow. "I guess we could leave now," she said in her turned-on voice.

Wes smirked. "Whatever you want, Kaylee. My body is yours to command."

CHAPTER TWENTY-TWO

Wes couldn't blame Kaylee for being gun-shy in terms of relationships. He'd failed her, and then McDouche had stepped in and really fucked things up. But this was Wes's second chance with the woman he'd never stopped loving. He was bringing his A-game.

Wes spotted Kaylee sitting at one of the poolside tables, smiling at the children in the water. He strode across the pavement and nudged out the chair beside her with his foot. He took a seat and held out two paper-wrapped sandwiches. "Ham or turkey?"

Kaylee grabbed the kettle chips he'd tucked under his arm. "You remembered!" Smiling, she ripped open the chip bag and gestured to the turkey sandwich.

He handed her the sandwich and sent her a look of disbelief. "You thought I'd forget your favorite junk food?" He inched his chair closer to hers as he scooted in. "I nearly received a severed arm the one time I took the last chip. That's not a lesson a man easily forgets." He feigned a shiver. "Never steal a woman's food when she's holding a knife."

Kaylee brought her hand to her mouth, covering her laugh and the food she was chewing. "Served you right! I would never steal the last red licorice. I can't believe you took that chip."

He shook his head. "You'll never get over it, will you?"

"No." But she was smiling.

Wes would make Kaylee laugh all day if he could. As far as he was concerned, when Kaylee was happy, flowers bloomed, strangers hugged, and road rage ceased to exist. He felt like he could conquer anything. But the tournament was around the corner, and Wes worried he'd fuck up what they had the same way he did in college.

Preparation for a tournament of that scale was massive, and he didn't want to ruin their budding relationship by being preoccupied. Not that Kaylee considered it a relationship. She was adamant about it being only sex. And he was happy to oblige. But the lunch dates he'd managed to slip in these last couple of weeks made it more than casual. Not that he planned to point that out to Kaylee. Wes made sure he took advantage of every free moment with her. Unfortunately, there weren't many.

He had been busting his ass getting things lined up for the big event, even putting aside practice sessions just so he could get his work done and still have time for Kaylee. It was a first. He'd never put anything ahead of golf.

Wes was willing to shove a few practices aside, but he couldn't let down his brothers when it came to keeping the club going. And the tournament was integral to keeping Club Tahoe flush after a shitty employee had embezzled money from them. It had happened right after they'd taken over running the place, and unfortunately, Club Tahoe lost important relationships with big business partners. They needed the tournament.

If only he could convince Kaylee that a relationship with him was the right thing. Then he could persuade her to hang tight until after the tournament, when they would be able to spend more time together. But she was being damned stubborn about this friends-with-benefits thing, making it a point to comment on how great it was.

Leave it to Kaylee to suddenly decide she didn't want anything more than sex.

Wes bit into his ham sandwich and studied her out of the corner of his eye. "So, I was thinking I could leave work a little early tonight. Barbecue for you. I've got steaks in the freezer that need to be cooked." That he'd picked up at the store after midnight last night on his way home to lure her to his lair. But she didn't need to know that. "What do you say?"

She nodded. "Yum. I'll bring a salad."

He shook his head. "Let me take care of everything."

She looked at him suspiciously. "I love spending time with you, but...you're not trying to woo me, are you?"

He chuckled and sat back in his chair, feigning a casual stance. "Cooking dinner for someone does not a relationship make."

"What's with the Yoda speak?"

God, he was nervous. And his dating skills were rusty. "I'm just saying, I got this. And don't worry; it's still only about sex."

Wes grabbed a chip and held it up for her approval. She smiled and nodded. He popped the chip in his mouth and wiped his fingers on a napkin. "Ask any of my brothers. I haven't wanted a relationship in years. Why would I start now?"

"Right. Yeah, okay."

Wes's mouth twisted. Her eyes had gone unfocused and she was kneading the top of her thigh.

Was she having second thoughts? Did she actually want a relationship but was too afraid to go for it?

Goddamn, taking things slow was annoying as hell.

Wes waited until Kaylee finished her sandwich. He grabbed the trash from the table and dumped it in the nearby canister.

Kaylee glanced at her phone and tucked it in her pocket. "I better get back. Hunt's watching the kids." She made a face. "If I leave him there for too long, I return to booby traps."

Wes grinned. "That sounds about right. So I'll pick you up at seven?"

"Sure."

Score. It was a date. Even if Kaylee didn't know it.

———

WES PICKED up Kaylee from her place and drove them to his one-room cabin off Pioneer Trail. She could have driven herself, but this way he got to spend more time with her. Plus, she'd been so busy trying to figure out if dinner meant something more, she hadn't complained when he said he'd pick her up.

Wes crossed the kitchen and grabbed another of Kaylee's favorite foods—cheese spread and crackers. He walked to the bar-height table and handed her them, along with a bottle of beer, while the steaks marinated.

He drummed his fingers and watched Kaylee slather her cracker with cheesy goodness, little moans erupting from her throat—getting him juiced up for other activities.

The table took up a quarter of the space in his place, the

bed nearly half. Which was fine, because that was where the magic happened. And if he was lucky, he'd get *lucky*. With the woman he—

Not *loved*.

Cared about. No need to go all crazy the way Adam had for Hayden, or even the way Levi was around Emily.

Jesus. Just because his older brothers were settling down, that didn't mean he had to do the permanent thing. Wes wanted to lock things down with Kaylee, sure, but not forever.

He frowned. If he didn't lock things down permanently with Kaylee, she'd date someone else...and that didn't sit well. Not. At. All.

He gave himself a sharp mental shake. Not going there. Still working on convincing her to call him her boyfriend.

"There's something that's been bothering me," he said, attempting to puzzle out her aversion to dating him in a serious way. He guessed their past was a strong influencer, but there had to be more. "You mentioned that McDouche—"

She rolled her eyes. "Eddy."

"—was there for you after we broke up."

She shook her head. "It was almost a year before I felt good enough to date, and then I met Eddy."

Wes's jaw clenched. He popped a cracker in his mouth, breathing deeply through his nose. Thinking of Kaylee going through all that medical stuff on her own made him want to break something. "Right. So, why did you date him and not some other guy? You never used to put up with idiots like *Eddy*."

She stole the cracker he'd spent several seconds spreading cheese on, and took a bite. "He was nice at first. And Eddy isn't hard on the eyes."

"If you're into that sort of thing," Wes grumbled.

"But you're right."

He looked up. "I am?"

She set the cracker down, and Wes brought his beer to his mouth, waiting impatiently for her to continue. "Eddy isn't the kind of guy I'd normally date. I think we connected because he can't have children either."

Wes choked on his beer. "Excuse me?"

She shrugged. "He suffered a lacrosse injury goofing around without proper gear. It severed his—"

Wes slammed down his bottle. "Stop. Right there. I don't need the details. Just hearing you mention balls and injury makes me queasy."

She shook her head, exasperated. "I never mentioned *balls*."

"It was implied."

She shrugged and popped the rest of the cracker in her mouth.

His hand formed a fist. He didn't know why her having this bond with Eddy pissed him off, but it did. "So you could relate to each other."

"Neither of us was going to be disappointed when the other couldn't have kids, so yeah, we could. At least, that's what I thought. But now... Now I'm not sure Eddy's the type of person to have children. I don't think his infertility meant as much to him as mine did to me. I almost wonder if he used it..."

"To get close to you?"

"Yes."

Considering the kind of guy Eddy was, Wes would bet his left nut it did. Not that he was willing to give up one of *his* boys.

"Sometimes..." She screwed her lips together.

"Sometimes?"

She took a gulp of beer. "Sometimes I wonder if he dated me because I was vulnerable and easy to manipulate. I was so desperate to connect with someone who understood what I was going through that I ignored problems in our relationship." She dropped her head in her hands. "I called a few of our mutual friends... Eddy had quite the harem going. I was such an idiot for not seeing what he was doing."

"Kaylee." He grabbed her hand, and she looked up. "Whatever he did, it wasn't your fault. That's who he is. It has nothing to do with you."

She nodded, but pulled her hand away slowly, wrapping her arms around her waist.

Wes stood and went to the fridge to grab Kaylee another beer. He replaced the one she'd almost finished. He should have never brought this up, but it did explain a lot. "So you were never on equal footing with this guy. And now you're afraid the same thing will happen with us."

Her body stiffened. "You walked all over me too."

He set his hands on the table and leaned down. "No, I didn't. You were always the most important thing to me. I was never with another woman. I've told you this."

"It didn't feel like equal footing the last six months we were together. There were obvious physical things going on with me. I was sick. And you had no idea."

"That was because I was an idiot. I've explained that."

She unlatched her arms from around her waist and straightened her back. "I'll never again put myself in a position where I'm not a priority."

"And you never should." He thought about the work he had ahead with the tournament, but pushed it aside. He could juggle Kaylee and his work schedule. He had to.

"You're right. I won't. Because I'll never let us go farther than we are now. I learned from our past." She gave him a shaky smile. "Friends with benefits, right?"

Fuck no, but he wasn't stupid enough to disagree with her. No matter what she said, they were a hell of a lot more than friends. "For now."

Before she could utter a response, he latched his mouth onto hers and kissed her until she was clinging to him. He lifted his mouth from her briefly. "There's more for us, Kaylee."

CHAPTER TWENTY-THREE

Wes was talking crazy. There wasn't more for them. It was too risky, and Kaylee wasn't sacrificing any part of herself she couldn't stand to lose. She wasn't budging on the relationship bit, and he'd figure that out soon enough.

Wes ran his hands down her shoulders and grabbed her elbows, urging her up.

"What about dinner?" she asked when his mouth had traveled to her neck. She angled her head back, because his lips felt incredible.

He guided her toward the massive bed, which was kind of hard to miss, given he lived in a shoebox.

Leave it to the trust fund kid to live in a five-hundred-square-foot cabin.

Considering the looks of his place, Wes's bed was the nicest thing he owned. But she couldn't complain, given she was currently receiving the benefits of his commitment to the bedroom.

The back of her knees hit the soft mattress and he ran his hands down her ribcage, dipping in at her waist and stopping at her hips. "I like the idea of having you in my bed."

So far they'd spent their sexy time at her place.

He picked her up a few inches off the ground and tossed her on the mattress.

"Wes!" she said, but she laughed and ducked for cover as he leapt onto her, supporting his weight with his arms.

"Yes, Kaylee?"

"We haven't eaten. I thought you were making me dinner."

He nuzzled her neck and did some sort of swirly thing with his tongue. "Oh, I plan to. But this is a brand-new mattress." He ran his hand seductively over the comforter, his mouth and face nuzzled in her neck as he murmured against her throat. "Breaking it in should be our first priority, don't you think?"

His hand homed in on her breast, and she grabbed his ass. She'd forgotten how fun and totally hot sex could be, until she and Wes started sneaking around Club Tahoe these last couple of weeks. "I like having sex with you," she said with a sigh.

He lifted his head and quirked an eyebrow, a grin on his face. "I like having sex with *you*." He kissed the tip of her nipple through her cotton shirt, sending a spark through her belly.

She pulled up his head by his silky, dark hair.

"Yes?" he said, drawing the word out, humor in his tone as he met her gaze.

"I mean, you make me feel beautiful. When we're together—" It was on the tip of her tongue to say that things felt right for the first time in years, but she couldn't say that. He'd read into it. She didn't want more than what they had right now. "You're special to me. That's all. I just wanted you to know that."

His grin faded. She was certain he was about to say something—probably about them being more than sex buddies—so she broke the spell and shoved him over.

Wes rolled easily onto his back and Kaylee climbed on top, straddling him.

His hands landed on her breasts. "Girl on top works for me."

Good thing Wes was easily distracted by boobs.

She let her hands roam his chest, content that the conversation hadn't veered too far in the wrong direction. She ran her palms down his stomach and under his T-shirt to the ridges of his muscled abs. She trailed her fingertips to his hipbones and teased them farther south, over the sculpted muscles that tapered into a V that was so totally hot.

Wes's body jerked—at least his erection did. He turned into a very malleable male when her hands were on him.

"Any farther south and I'll be flipping you over," he said. "But don't let that stop you from your exploration." He folded his arms behind his head and grinned as she unhooked her bra. And then his hands were on her breasts again and his expression had gone serious. "I will love these forever, Kaylee. They're mine."

She laughed. "You're ridiculous."

"The only thing ridiculous is that your pants are still on."

Ignoring him, she flipped the button of his jeans, unzipped his fly, and slid his pants down to the tops of his thighs.

His gaze turned half-lidded. "Don't stop. Please don't

stop. I'll give you oral five times a day if you'll just keep going."

"That's not a bargain. You'd do that anyway."

"True." His eyes flared. "I love the taste of you."

A streak of arousal hit her where it counted and she slid down his body, suddenly eager for what she had in mind. "I remember the way you taste too." She pulled out his thick, long erection, and he groaned as she stroked him. "And feel in my mouth." She sent him a naughty grin.

Wes stared, hardly blinking as she ran her tongue over the top of his erection. She took him in as far as she could go, swirling her tongue and sucking him.

His breathing increased and his hands balled at his sides. *"Fuck."*

His head dropped back, and she watched him while she stroked him. Would have been smiling too at how much he seemed to be enjoying this, if her mouth weren't so busy. She wasn't kidding when she'd said she thought he'd grown. Wes was big. Or bigger than she'd been used to these last few years.

Kaylee worked the length of him with her hands and her mouth and her tongue, until she felt her body being lifted.

Wes pulled her up and flipped her over, covering her. And then his mouth was on hers, hot with hunger.

Kaylee hadn't stopped loving Wes—might never stop. But that didn't mean she trusted him with her heart. It wasn't the wisest thing to have sex with him when she had no intention of going farther, but she couldn't help herself. He was persuasive, and she cared deeply for him.

He stopped kissing her only to remove their clothes quickly and efficiently. And then he was inside her, staring into her eyes as though he cherished and loved her.

If anyone had asked Kaylee four years ago what it took to have a good relationship, she would have described this. Not the sex, but the way Wes looked at her, wanted to be with her, touched her with such devotion. But she was older and wiser now. She needed more than what he was currently offering. Needed to be someone's priority.

Wes wasn't dating anyone else—Kaylee knew him well enough to trust him to be monogamous—but she wasn't sure she could trust him after he'd put his professional aspirations above her the last time they'd dated. And therein lay the problem. She *wanted* Wes to accomplish his dreams—had always wanted that for him. It was why she'd let things go on as long as she had in college without complaining. But in the end, putting her needs aside had almost destroyed her.

She wouldn't risk it.

"You're distracted." He frowned. "What the hell could you be thinking about at a moment like this? I'm about to explode, but I need you to come first."

"I'm thinking about you."

His eyes narrowed. "Better be about how close you are to coming." He flipped them over until she was on top again. His thumb touched the apex of her thighs, swirling a slow and steady rhythm against the pulse beating there.

She moaned and pressed her hands to his chest, rocking on him and letting the sensation bring her higher. He was hitting her in the right spot, and every time she dropped down, pleasure swirled through her. Her muscles contracted and a cry escaped her throat.

Wes let her ride it out, and then his hands gripped her hips as he thrust inside her. He came seconds later, his movements slowing, chest heaving.

Kaylee curled up on him, feeling the pounding of his heart as his body came down.

"Coming inside you never gets old."

"I'm glad you're happy," she said, but Kaylee was convinced she got more out of this new form of a relationship than Wes did. He was so eager to please her, and what girl could turn that down?

He pressed his large palm to her lower back and tucked her close. "Why wouldn't I be happy? Spending time with you is always good: laughing, having sex on the golf course, watching you take care of the tyrants known as children at Club Kids. And you fit exactly right against my body. Nothing could be better."

She closed her eyes. Why was he being the perfect guy now when she was so leery? "You're a great guy, Wes."

His stilled and then said, "I'm great for you."

CHAPTER TWENTY-FOUR

Wes realized he'd been pushing things a little hard in the get-Kaylee-to-be-my-girl department. He eased back. But only just. He'd stopped talking about how great they were for each other and focused on showing her. So far, she seemed more relaxed, to the point that she'd stopped worrying about what anyone thought and allowed him to bring her around as though they were dating. Even though technically—*according to her*—they weren't.

"Are you sure you want me to go?" Kaylee asked as they got dressed at her place. They'd gone to her parents' cabin after work to get cleaned up.

Fine, she'd gone home to get cleaned up, and he'd gone to seduce her in the shower.

"Of course." Wes pulled a T-shirt over his head, followed by a long-sleeved Henley. "The tournament week begins tomorrow and we're going over final details. No heavy drinking. We all need to be on our game in the morning."

"And are you on your game?" she asked as she slipped

on low boots with her jeans. "You haven't been practicing as much. Does that worry you?"

He gave her a mock frown. "I wasn't nervous until you mentioned it."

She grinned. "Sorry. It's just, this is what you've always wanted."

He sank onto her bed and tied his shoes. "It was. But I like working at the club." He chuckled. "Never thought I'd say that. When I first stepped up my role at the golf course after our father died, I was crawling out of my skin to get away. Sounds strange, but everything changed when I started giving lessons to Bella."

He finished with his shoes and leaned on his thighs. "It was amazing to see a little kid kill it out there. That was true talent. I've always been athletic, but Bella's got magic. For once, I was excited for someone else's career. Teaching Bella made me realize how rewarding training could be. I still don't get much out of teaching people with no skill, however."

"Like me."

He flashed her a naughty grin. "*You* are an exception."

"Because I get naked with you?"

"Exactly."

She tossed a throw pillow at his head. "You're bad."

He deflected the pillow with an exaggerated karate move. "Anyway. As I was saying, before I was so rudely interrupted. It might have taken the tragedy of my father passing for me to try something new, but it was a wake-up call. I'm not kidding myself with this sponsor's exemption. It's an incredible opportunity, but it's not going to result in a tour career. I've never consistently scored low enough to make it on the circuit. I'm going to go out there and have the time of my life, but I've got other dreams I'm focusing on now."

"Training little Bella?"

He stood and pulled Kaylee up with him. "Training Bella and others like her is one of them." He kissed her on the lips and grabbed her hand before she could ask him about his other dreams.

Kaylee didn't want to know his ideas for them. But someday, hopefully soon, she would. "Come on. They're waiting for us. We better go."

———

"TELL me again why we're meeting at Blue Casino instead of the Fireside Lounge?" Kaylee scanned the casino floor. Neon blue with orange accents decorated the loud gaming area.

Adam and his new wife Hayden worked at Blue in management, but they'd only just returned from their honeymoon. Kaylee didn't think Hayden had gone back to work yet, and she'd heard Adam was helping Levi and Emily with the tournament all week. She wasn't sure if it was a conflict of interest for Adam to work at Blue Casino and to be a part owner of Club Tahoe, but clearly Blue didn't seem to mind.

Wes placed his hand at the small of her back as she walked up the few steps to the Monte Belle lounge, where his brothers and their significant others were waiting. "It's two-for-one beers until seven tonight. We couldn't pass it up."

She scanned his face. "Are you serious? You guys are probably the richest men in town and you're bargain drinking?"

"Who doesn't like a good two-for-one?"

She threw up her hands. "Apparently, not even billionaires."

"Not sure billionaire is accurate. Multimillions, possibly. Haven't checked the trust in over a decade."

She tripped on the carpet. "Excuse me?"

Wes stopped and turned his back to his brothers. "You know I never cared about that stuff."

"I know you never cared if others had money, and I know you're not a snob. But who doesn't know how much they have?"

He scratched the back of his neck. "I know how much *I* have, just not how much my father put into a trust for me. That was always his money."

"And he gave it to you. Wes, there are people struggling out there who would kill for a fraction of what your father gave you. If you don't want it, donate it."

He sighed. "I hear you, and I'll consider it. Right now, Levi is pulling from all of our trust funds to keep things moving at the resort. Afterward...I'll consider what to do next."

She wrapped her hand around his thick upper arm, and they continued walking toward the group. This was Wes. The multimillionaire who lived in a simple one-room cabin and went to two-for-one beer nights. He wasn't materialistic. He wasn't a cheater. And he cared about her. He was a man who was making it damn hard to not fall in love with him again.

She sighed and put on a smile for the larger-than-normal group tonight.

Emily stood and gave Kaylee a hug. "I'm so glad you guys could make it." She looked at Kaylee and waggled her eyebrows with a glance at Wes.

"We're friends," Kaylee said quietly, reading Emily's mind. All of Wes's brothers and their significant others had made assumptions about Kaylee and Wes, but she refused to define their relationship.

"*Anyway*," Emily said, clearly not believing her. "Let me introduce you to a few of our friends. This is Jaeg and his fiancée Cali, along with Cali's cousin, Ireland. Ireland just started working at Blue Casino."

The pretty redhead, sitting next to Jaeg's fiancée, waved. "Nice to meet you." Her gaze skittered to Bran.

Poor Bran. Personally, Kaylee thought Wes was the most handsome Cade, but there were some women who couldn't take their eyes off Bran. Unfortunately, Wes's brother was seriously shy.

Kaylee and Wes greeted the rest of the group and took seats at the three round tables pushed together to accommodate everyone. Wes's brothers were pretty big guys. Add Jaeg to the mix, and it was like a table of quarterbacks.

"So what's the plan for tomorrow?" Kaylee asked. "What can I do to help? Keep the kids away?"

"Actually," Emily said, "I was thinking we could bring them. Most of the parents in town will be at the event. We might not have many kids at Club Kids that day, but the ones who are there can enjoy the tournament. Adam is our extra pair of hands for the week." She turned to Adam, who had his arm around Hayden's waist and appeared completely in love with his new wife. "You don't mind putting together a picnic for Club Kids, do you?"

"I'm at your service."

Hayden smiled up at him. "I'll help too. I'm taking tomorrow off. Blue knows we aren't mentally back from our honeymoon, and they're giving us tons of leeway this week."

"Excellent," Emily said. "So with the kids taken care of,

the merchandise and corporate tents ready to go, the food vendors and restaurants prepared"—she looked at Bran, who nodded—"the golf course and tournament people lined up, thanks to Wes and Levi... We should be good. Unless something goes wrong. Which it always does." She sank her forehead onto her hand and closed her eyes. Levi rubbed her back.

"Is she okay?" Kaylee asked.

"She's fine," Levi said. Emily lifted her hand, waving in agreement. "She's just stressed."

"But you're not?"

Levi shrugged. "Emily stresses enough for the both of us. It's my job to keep her calm."

Wes snorted and Kaylee looked at him.

"He means in the bedroom," Wes said.

Levi shot Wes a scowl.

"Is there anything we can do to help?" Cali asked.

"This is major," Jaeg said. "We should be on hand tomorrow as well."

"Absolutely," Cali agreed. "Actually, I wouldn't be surprised if my boss and the entire construction crew took the week off to enjoy the tournament. It's not often something like this comes into town."

Wes had told Kaylee on the way over about the friends joining them tonight. Apparently, Cali worked for one of Jaeg and Adam's friends, who owned a local construction company.

"And me too. I'll be there," Ireland chimed in. This time she didn't glance at Bran, but Kaylee caught Bran frown anyway.

He really didn't like this girl. And that made no sense. She was very pretty, and seemed sweet.

"I'm here for the foreseeable future," Ireland said. "I'd

love to get more involved."

Bran grumbled lightly.

Ireland's shoulders stiffened at the sound, but she tried to smile. "I've worked in just about every field as I paid my way through college and graduate school, so I come experienced."

Bran glanced over, and this time, there was a hint of surprise on his face. Maybe even admiration. But it quickly faded and he looked back at his brothers. "So long as we don't have any food-poisoning incidents, all should go well."

"Are you kidding?" Hunt said. He'd been checking his phone nonstop. "Anything can go wrong, and probably will."

Emily sucked in a breath, her eyes widening.

Levi scowled. "Shut it, Hunt. You're not helping."

"In that case," Hunt said, "we done here? I've got plans." He scanned Ireland. "Feel free to join me. No need to stick around with the couples."

Ireland blushed and glanced at Bran. "Not everyone has a significant other."

Hunt shook his head. "Who, Bran? You won't find him with a woman."

"I'm with plenty of women," Bran grumbled. "Just not the kind you go out with." He looked at Ireland, as though she were an example.

Her face turned bright red to match her hair. She looked away and said, "No thank you. I'm hanging out with my cousin tonight."

Cali bumped Ireland's shoulder in solidarity.

Ouch. Bran's comment and the look he shot Ireland? Harsh.

Ireland was really pretty. Striking, even, with her bright red hair and fair skin. She was also curvy. So basically, the kind of woman most guys drooled over. Come to think of it, Kaylee would expect Wes to drool over her too, but he was busy trying to inch his hand up Kaylee's thigh. He also kept leaning in and sniffing her hair.

"You smell good," he whispered in his sexy, low voice.

Wes was a menace; they'd just had sex! But Kaylee smiled. She'd never had to worry about him with other women. Once he settled, he was a one-woman guy.

And then her smile died. Had he settled?

They were having sex. And though it seemed he'd been free with his affections before she'd arrived in town, she'd not seen him with anyone since. He'd confirmed it when he said as much. And now they were having sex in a friends-with-benefits sort of way.

Okay, so the lines of relationship and sex buddies had thinned. But if he hadn't been a one-woman kind of guy, she wouldn't have agreed to the arrangement.

Adam waved at the waitress in the lounge, who seemed to be waiting for his signal. A couple of the guys were drinking beers, but some had opted for bottles of water.

The waitress came over with several small yellow shot glasses.

"Lemon drops," Levi said. "Emily's choice, since she single-handedly orchestrated the tour bringing in hundreds of workers, hired fifty new employees, and got the casino and hotel primed for the event. Bran and I simply bumped around as urban Sherpas, hauling things and cracking skulls when needed."

Hunt held up a glass, and everyone else did too. "Kind of a fruity shot, but I'm game. To Emily for saving us, to Wes kicking ass on the course tomorrow, and to no one getting stampeded by the crowd."

"Cheers," they all said.

CHAPTER TWENTY-FIVE

The first day of the tournament came and went in a haze of activity. Not only did the hotel and casino pull it off while Wes was busy playing the round of his life, but Wes made it into the top twenty-five with a score of four under. And it didn't end there. The days to follow were even better.

There was no way in hell Wes could have predicted he'd make it past the first round with such a high placement on the leaderboard. He was even more surprised to make the cut after the second day, beating half the pros. And now he was halfway through the final round of the tournament in the top ten, with a legitimate chance of finishing high enough to get an exemption into the next tournament.

It was mind-blowing.

He scanned the bleachers. He'd been so focused today that this was the first moment he'd had a chance to look for Kaylee. Not that he had any hope of seeing her. She'd been busy with the kids all weekend, and the buzz of having a local boy near the top in the final round drew even larger crowds.

Wes should have been nervous. He had been at the beginning of the tournament, but taking over the running of the golf course changed him. He had other dreams to focus on besides golf championships.

Dreams like running a children's golf program. Like being with Kaylee.

Life was good with or without being at the top of his favorite sport, but he wasn't complaining, because this was incredible.

He putted in another birdie on the second-to-last hole and picked up his ball, glancing once more at the bleachers. Still no sign of Kaylee.

Thank fuck the event had gone well so far. They'd experienced one minor incident, with the club running out of pool and beach towels, but Levi had rented a massive truck and sent Jaeg to two different Costcos for backups. Turned out, after people had been on the course all day, their next move was to hit the pool. Late night gambling followed. There were two situations Wes heard about where spectators got into brawls. Adam took care of it, though, by reaching out to his connections at Blue Casino for extra off-duty guard help.

They'd hired additional security, but apparently some golf fans could be assholes when they drank and became hyped from the competition. Not that Wes could blame them. He was the most competitive of his brothers. Which was why it was such a surprise to find that when he focused his competitive streak on something else—like, say, a sassy brunette—it left him room to just play the game.

Amazing. He should have brought Kaylee to all of his golf events in college.

But he hadn't. He'd been a selfish dick. He thought he

had the girl, and all he'd needed was to get on the pro tour. God, he'd been an idiot.

Wes followed his caddy and the crowd to the last hole. No time like the present to stay on course—the course being to make Kaylee as happy as possible. He only wished he could let her know she was the most important thing to him. Because she was, he'd realized.

After Kaylee told him about the miscarriage and why she'd left him, he'd decided they'd not been given a fair chance with all that had happened. Yes, he'd made mistakes, but his heart had always been with her. Now he just needed to convince her they were right for each other.

It wasn't until Wes was about to make his last putt that he finally caught a glimpse of Kaylee. She was smiling behind the eighteenth green with her arms wrapped around the shoulders of two kids. She stole his breath. And a good thing too. He was so focused on how amazing she was, he'd subconsciously lined up his putt, and then calmly rolled the ball into the hole for yet another birdie.

Wes ran a hand down his face, smiling. The tournament was over, and he'd made it into the top ten. Which meant he automatically qualified for the next tournament.

Holy fuck.

WES HANDED in his scorecard and headed straight for Kaylee. And got tackled by an excited Bella.

"You did it, Wes! You did it!"

"You're going to be out there too someday, Bella."

"With hard work, right? Just like you tell me."

"That's exactly right." He set her down and shook her parents' hands. They were equally excited, and appeared genuinely grateful for the work Wes had put into helping their daughter learn the game.

Maybe her parents weren't so bad after all, and he was glad to know it. Wes watched Bella walk away holding hands with her father, her mother smiling beside them.

He searched for Kaylee, but she seemed to have wandered off in the excitement. She was still working and in charge of at least a couple of kids. She must have taken them back to Club Kids. His shoulders slumped. He wanted to celebrate with her, but he understood she had a job to do.

The next blow to his body came from Hunt, who nearly knocked him over. "Fuck you. I can't believe it," Hunt said excitedly. "You asshole. You never told us there was a chance you'd do well."

"I didn't know either." Wes chuckled. "It's as much a shock to me as it is to you."

Soon he ran into all of his brothers as well as Jaeg, Cali, and a few other friends, who all congratulated him. His family couldn't talk long, as they were on duty until the last tournament guest left the grounds, but it meant a lot to Wes to have them close during the tournament of his life.

He checked in with his second-in-command of the golf program, as well as the head groundskeeper. All was going well, and sales of clubs were at an all-time high, something they hadn't anticipated. Wes had figured they'd sell a boatload of T-shirts, but not clubs.

It wasn't until dusk that he finally spotted Kaylee walking toward him from the direction of the resort. She was kid-less, which meant she was off work.

He jogged toward her and picked her up, taking her mouth with his.

He swung her around, and she tilted her head back laughing. "Put me down before you make me barf!"

Wes gently set her on the ground, not caring what a sap he looked like. "Can you believe it?"

She grinned from ear to ear. "Yes. I knew you could do it."

Wes wasn't the kind of guy to get choked up. Pretty much never did unless one of his stupid brothers turned on the waterworks, which was almost never. But he had to fight back the heat burning behind his eyes.

He buried his head near her neck and breathed in her scent. "Thank you for always believing in me. Even when I was an oblivious ass."

"You were twenty-two. Most twenty-two-year-olds are oblivious asses. I forgave you a long time ago. Just needed you to forgive me for how I handled things."

He straightened and held her close. "Nothing to forgive." He'd said it before, but he'd say it again. "I'm always here for you. From here on out, okay?"

She studied his eyes, and for the first time, he thought he might be getting through to her. That she might be looking at him in a different light. One that could mean a future for them.

"Wes Cade?"

Wes looked over his shoulder at a man walking toward them.

He'd run into his buddy Tom, who'd hooked them up with the Tahoe Invitational, but Wes hadn't met any of the lead organizers. He'd been too busy playing. And the way this guy was dressed in a navy blazer with a red patch appeared official.

"I'm Wes." He shook the guy's hand and introduced Kaylee.

"Great playing out there," the tour official said. "Didn't know our host was so good at the game." He leaned closer as though imparting a secret. "Most people who take the sponsor's exemption aren't."

Wes chuckled. "To be honest, I had a few good days. That was all."

"Really good days, from what I've seen." He turned to Kaylee. "Nice to meet you, ma'am. Wes, be sure to get in touch after the tournament. We loved your course. I want to talk about future opportunities if you're interested."

"Absolutely. Thank you, sir."

Kaylee was silent as the man walked away, but as soon as he was out of earshot, she squeezed him around the waist. "Holy shit, Wes! This is your chance."

He nodded. Everything he'd ever wanted was coming together. But he was also trying to figure out how he'd keep all the balls in the air—this next tournament, working at the club, and Kaylee. As soon as he'd made her a priority, things had started to come together. But how the hell was he going to accept all the good being thrown at him and not drop something?

CHAPTER TWENTY-SIX

Two weeks had passed since the Tahoe Invitational, and Wes had been gone nearly the entire time. His scores came in strong at the next tournament, so Wes arrived home for a couple of days, then left for the following tournament as well. He missed Kaylee like crazy, but she was being great about the travel and supporting his dream.

Wes pulled into his driveway and Kaylee came running out of the cabin and into his arms. "Hi," she said casually.

"Hi?" He grabbed her ass and carried her into the house, shutting the door with his foot. "I've been gone for five days and all I get is a hi?" He dropped his bag by the door and carried her over to the bed, bringing them down on top of the mattress. "I missed you." He breathed in her scent and ran his hands down her body.

"I missed you too, but I didn't want you to feel bad about being gone. Wanted you to have this."

"Don't ever hold back from telling me how much you miss me. Matter of fact, you can show me." He grabbed her breast, and she winced. "Did I hurt you?"

Her cute nose wrinkled. "I'm fine. My boobs are just ridiculously sore this month. Stupid PMS."

He dipped his head and barely touched her breast in a light kiss. "Better?"

She ran her hand up and down his erection. "Only my boobs are sore. No need to go all gentle with the rest of me." She squeezed his ass.

He leaned back in mock horror. "I'm shocked. I thought you were a delicate flower."

She laughed, and he started pulling off her pants and nibbling down her belly. "I missed these panties." He tugged them off with his teeth. "And these sexy legs." He licked her thigh up to the crease, and she ran her hand in his hair, clenching it.

"Hurry up, Wes. Do you know how long it's been?"

He whipped off his shirt. "Five days, six hours, and forty-two minutes."

She leaned up on her elbows as he shucked off his pants. "Really?"

He lifted one shoulder and lay beside her, his gaze focused on her breasts—which apparently were off-limits. "I was bored on the plane and decided to calculate how long it had been since I'd seen you. Now, where were we? Oh yes, I'm not allowed to put my mouth on your breasts. I guess I'll have to settle for licking other areas." He quirked his eyebrow and her chest rose.

"With your magic tongue?"

"My magic tongue is very"—he kissed her nose, then her lips—"very restless."

And that was how they spent the night. Making up for lost time. In bed. Eating. Laughing. And finally falling asleep.

At ten the next morning, Wes yawned and looked over

at Kaylee. She was lying very still, but she wasn't asleep. She also wasn't smiling or rolling into him like she normally did when she first woke. "You okay?"

"I don't feel well. I think my body is trying to fight off something."

He sat up, but kept the covers tucked around her. "Do you want me to call Emily? Tell her you're not going in tomorrow?"

She shook her head and clutched her stomach. "No. I think it'll pass, but I might stay in your bed for the day, if that's all right?"

He kissed her forehead. "Stay as long as you like. I've got to run into work and make sure the course is okay. I'll be back in a few hours. Do you want me to get you anything?"

She mumbled, "No," and burrowed deeper under the covers.

Wes showered and dressed. He made toast and coffee for the both of them. When he looked over at Kaylee, she was still buried under the covers. "You should eat something."

She moaned.

He moved to the bed and sat on the edge, resting his hand on her leg. "Kaylee, are you really okay?"

She peeked out from beneath the covers and gave him a weak smile. "I'm feeling a little better." She sat up and reached for the T-shirt he'd discarded the night before.

She eased out of bed and padded over to the table where he'd left the toast. Climbing onto the barstool, she tucked his shirt beneath her bottom, then took a bite of the buttered toast. "This is good. I think I just needed food."

Kaylee was adorable with her hair ruffled and wearing his shirt. He'd never get tired of this sight. "I'll bring you whatever you want. Just give me a call if anything sounds good. You know Bran will hook you up from one of the restaurants."

She grinned and waved. "Don't worry about me. Good luck getting caught up with work. Do they know you're leaving again tomorrow?"

He shook his head. "I planned to tell them once I got there."

"How will you do it? Run the golf course and be on the pro tour."

He grabbed his keys and ran a hand down his face. It had all happened so fast. First he was planning the Tahoe Invitational, expecting to play in it and nothing more, and then he was on the pro tour. "I never thought I'd have to. But it's the opportunity of a lifetime. I can't give it up, you know?"

She swallowed, and for a split second, he saw doubt on her face. And then she smiled. "You shouldn't." She picked up another piece of toast but didn't bite into it, just held it in her hand and studied it as if it were the most interesting thing she'd seen in days.

Wes walked over and kissed the back of her head. "I'll be back soon."

But once he was outside, he started having second thoughts. He couldn't fuck things up with Kaylee. So far, she'd been great about everything. And no man in his right mind would pass up the opportunity to play on the pro tour. It had to be good enough for now.

Wes climbed in his Range Rover and headed for the club.

———

LEVI AND BRAN had met Wes in the Club Tahoe steakhouse for lunch. "Kaylee's not feeling well," Wes said.

Levi frowned. "What do you mean she's not feeling well? Did you do something?"

"Course not." Wes took a bite of garlic bread. "She's got an upset stomach or something." He chewed the bread, his brow furrowing. "Should I be worried? Make her see a doctor?"

Levi looked to Bran, and Bran shrugged. "You're asking us?"

Good point. What did his brothers know?

Wes didn't feel right about leaving Kaylee at the house when she wasn't feeling well. But he'd been gone for two weeks and was about to leave for another week. His brothers would have killed him if he didn't check in today. He'd been running things remotely, and it was a load on everyone to put up with his absence.

"Wes," Levi said, "you're going to have to make a decision soon. Take this tour thing seriously, or commit to the club. You can't do both. But just so you know, if you screw things up with Kaylee and in any way cause her to leave us, Emily will bring down the wrath of hell on you."

Wes leaned back. "Damn. You had to go there, didn't you?"

Levi grinned. "I know how frightened you are of my girlfriend."

Wes nodded sagely. "I don't like to make the velvet hammer angry."

Bran chuckled.

"Exactly," Levi said. "And Emily loves Kaylee. The club also needs Kaylee for Club Kids. *So don't fuck it up.*"

"Already telling myself that, brother."

———————

CHAPTER TWENTY-SEVEN

Kaylee could feel Emily staring. "Do I have something on my face?"

Emily shook her head as she gestured for the workmen to bring the boxes for the new indoor climbing wall into the Club Kids play zone. "No, it's just you look pale. And...I heard you in the bathroom this morning. Is everything okay?"

Crap. Kaylee had been feeling nauseated lately, but it was this thing that came and went. Wes had left a couple of days ago and she was feeling better. Every once in a while, though, her stomach cramped and she felt like she was going to be sick. This morning she'd forgotten to eat breakfast, and she did get sick. That must have been when Emily walked into the bathroom. The feeling had passed as soon as she ate a few crackers from the pool bar.

Kaylee told the men which wall they were to build the structure on, waited until they started setting up, then turned back to Emily. "I've had the new assistant working with the kids while I focus on the other projects. Club Kids has thinned out since the tournament, but I can stay home if you think it best. It's just... I'm not sure what's wrong. I don't have a fever, only this occasional nausea."

Emily gently grabbed Kaylee's arm and pulled her aside. "Kaylee, I don't want to pry. I get the sense you and Wes don't like talking about your—friendship. But is it possible you're pregnant?"

Kaylee stared. That was probably exactly how this looked from the outside. "No. Absolutely not." She shook her head.

"Have you checked?"

Kaylee swallowed. She never thought about pregnancy. Not since her hometown doctor had told her she'd never be able to get pregnant. And Kaylee hadn't used precautions with Eddy.

But Eddy couldn't have kids...

"Kaylee? Are you okay?"

"I— Yeah, sorry. I just—it's not something I considered because I was told I couldn't have children." The doctor's words had seemed so final at the time. But without a haze of depression washing over her, she wondered if the doctor could have been wrong. She'd never gotten a second opinion.

Emily closed her eyes. "I'm so sorry I brought it up. I didn't know."

"No, it's fine. But really, I just have a touch of some bug. I need to make sure I eat breakfast. I forgot this morning, and that seemed to make it worse."

Emily cocked her head to the side. "You know, my sister just got pregnant. She said if she doesn't eat before she gets out of bed, she feels ill. Do you think it's some sort of hormone thing?"

Kaylee chuckled. "I have no idea, but I'll see a doctor and have it checked out. Promise."

Emily smiled. "Let me know if you need me to cover for you. After working eighty-hour weeks leading up to the Tahoe Invitational, I suddenly have all this time on my hands."

"Thank you. I'll let you know. I'm still new to the area, so I don't even have a doctor."

Emily pulled out her phone. "I'll send you my doctor contacts as well as my sister's local OB/GYN. If it's something that has to do with hormones, you'll need one."

Kaylee thanked Emily and made a few calls later that day to see about scheduling an appointment. Everyone was booked, but Club Tahoe had nice health benefits, even for the local urgent care. She'd swing by before heading home just to make sure whatever bug she had wasn't contagious, if nothing else.

———

KAYLEE DROVE HOME from the urgent care clinic, shaking her head. "They're wrong. Had to be some mistake."

Her phone buzzed on the seat beside her and she jumped. She stopped at a stoplight and glanced at the caller ID.

Wes. Naturally, he'd call when she was completely freaking out.

The phone rang again, and she pulled over. "Hello?"

"What are you wearing?"

"That's how you greet me?"

"You said you only want me for my body. I'm sticking with our script."

She laughed. Despite the sudden *what the fuck* moment

she was experiencing, this man could always make her laugh. "I said I didn't want anything serious."

"Exactly. All sex, all the time."

"Our non-relationship has caused inflation damage to your ego. We might need to deflate that a bit."

"Can I help it if I'm a confident man?"

Confident? God, the night they had sex on the golf course, he'd joked that he might have gotten her pregnant with his explosive make-up orgasm. He couldn't have been right. Yet according to the doctor she'd just seen—Wes was right.

Kaylee was pregnant.

She swallowed. "Were you calling for a reason, or to bug me while I'm driving?"

"Are you driving? You shouldn't answer the phone when you're on the road."

"I *was* driving. Now I'm on the side of the road waiting for you to tell me why you called twice, making me worry there's some kind of emergency."

"I'll make it quick, because I don't like the idea of you on the side of a dark road. Guess who's earned enough in the last few tournaments to qualify for the rest of the tournaments this season?"

"Wes Cade, up-and-coming golf star?"

"That's right, beautiful. You ready to travel the world with me?"

Her heart sank. *Not again.*

She had a job she loved in Lake Tahoe. New friends. A new life. And now she was supposedly pregnant... She still couldn't believe that last one. And he was asking her to give it up? He was excited and didn't know all the facts, but it felt like before.

The last time Kaylee had built her life around Wes, it had imploded. She couldn't risk it.

"First of all, congratulations. You're an incredible athlete, and you've worked hard for this. Second, we'll have to talk about the other stuff when you get home. When are you coming home?"

"Sunday, as soon as the tournament is over. But seriously, Kaylee. We joke about things being casual between us, but they aren't for me, and I don't think they are for you either. I want more." He let out a deep sigh. "The last thing I want is to force you to quit your job the way that douche you were engaged to did, but this is the opportunity of a lifetime and I want you with me. Just consider the travel, okay?"

Consider changing her life for him? This was exactly why she'd not wanted anything serious with Wes. Because she'd be tempted to do whatever it took to be with this man. That was how it had always been. She'd kept things casual between them, but she couldn't lie to herself and say she didn't love him. Kaylee had always loved Wes. Too much. That was the problem. She tended to put her needs aside.

"A cop car is about to pull up." A lie. She needed an excuse to not answer the question. "I gotta go. Talk to you later?"

"Sure." But she heard the hesitation in his tone. He knew her too well.

What was she going to do?

CHAPTER TWENTY-EIGHT

T hrough some intricate Tahoe connection, Emily got Kaylee an appointment with her sister's OB/GYN the next day. Kaylee hadn't told Emily the reason for her need to see the specialist, only that the urgent care doctor said it was important she go.

Pregnancy was a big deal. Especially when a person was told they couldn't get pregnant.

The physician at the urgent care had to have been mistaken.

"Well," the doctor said, folding her hands in her lap, "I've told you that the over-the-counter pregnancy test they gave you at the urgent care clinic is highly accurate. After the physical exam and a quick ultrasound, I can confirm your pregnancy."

Kaylee's jaw unhinged.

"I saw the scar tissue the previous doctor noted. In my opinion, it wouldn't have been enough to prevent future pregnancies, which is why you're pregnant now. I'm sorry they gave you such a dire prognosis and left you unprepared. From what I can tell, your pregnancy is progressing just fine. Would you like to hear the baby's heartbeat?"

Baby. *Baby.*

Kaylee couldn't speak. Couldn't form words. She simply nodded.

The doctor grabbed the ultrasound wand and placed it back on Kaylee's lower tummy with light pressure. She pressed a button—and Kaylee heard the rhythmic sound of her child's heartbeat.

Her and Wes's child.

She started crying. "This can't be."

A warm hand gently landed on her shoulder. "It's real," the doctor said. She turned toward the screen and made small movements with the wand on Kaylee's belly. "You're about ten weeks, according to these measurements."

Kaylee sat up abruptly. "Ten weeks!"

The doctor smiled. "Ten weeks. I'd like you to start taking prenatal vitamins right away. There's a small list of other things I want you to consider while you're pregnant—foods to avoid, that sort of thing. There are several pregnancy books out there to help you deal with the changes going on inside your body. But in the meantime, do you have any questions for me?"

"Yes. What do I do?"

The doctor laughed. "Take care of yourself. Get plenty of rest. Stay hydrated and eat healthy. Exercise as you normally would, and if exercise isn't something you typically do, you might consider taking walks at least once a day."

The doctor put the ultrasound wand away and gave Kaylee tissues to wipe the gel off her stomach. "Have you told the father?"

"No." Kaylee shook her head in a daze. "I didn't even

know this was a possibility. My periods are irregular, and with the scar tissue..."

"Understandable. I'm happy to meet with him as well if you want to schedule another time to come in. Otherwise, I'd like to see you in four weeks. You can schedule the appointment at the front desk."

The doctor gave Kaylee forms to fill out and left her to get dressed. Kaylee walked out of the exam room and scheduled her next appointment.

She exited the building, walking blindly to her car, where she sat. And stared out the windshield. One moment, tears streamed down her cheeks and she smiled. The next moment, panic tightened her chest and she was crying for a different reason.

She breathed in and out slowly, attempting to calm down. Stress wasn't healthy, and she had a *baby* growing inside her.

What the hell was she going to tell Wes?

Wes's dreams were coming true. Dreams that not only took him away from Kaylee, but would take him away from their child—if this pregnancy didn't end in miscarriage like the first.

God, *miscarriage.*

She shook her head. Couldn't think about that right now. She had to focus on telling Wes. She wouldn't make the same mistake twice and leave him in the dark. He deserved to know, regardless of how he might take it.

He was a good man. An even better man than when she'd dated him before—and she'd loved him to stupid levels back then. Only what if she told him about the baby and he quit the tour? And gave up the only dream he'd ever wanted?

———

KAYLEE WAS UPSTAIRS when Wes called out her name. He must have used her hide-a-key, the bugger.

"Up here!" She quickly shoved the pregnancy book her doctor had recommended under the bed and crossed her legs, brushing back her hair.

She heard him bound up the stairs and cross the hall to the master bedroom. He stood in the doorway.

Wes was beaming, happier than she'd ever seen him. He dropped his bag, crossed the room, and crawled onto the bed. He wrapped his arms around her waist and used her stomach as a pillow. Right above their baby.

Kaylee blinked back tears that all of a sudden flooded her eyes. Damn pregnancy hormones. She couldn't start crying. It was critical they had this conversation without her showing too much emotion and guilt-tripping Wes into doing something he'd regret.

Wes let out a long sigh, his entire body going lax and heavy. "I missed you. So happy to be home."

Were they a home? The two of them together?

He looked up sleepily. Poor guy had been traveling nonstop. "How are you feeling? You've been fighting that bug for a couple of weeks now, right? Have you gone to see someone about it?"

She nodded.

"And?"

"I'm healthy." She didn't know why she didn't just tell him then. She was allowing her fears to get the best of her.

"Good. So have you thought about what I said over the phone?" He sounded super excited. "About you traveling with me? Levi will kick my ass if I take you away from the club, but whatever. He can deal."

She looked at him sadly. "I can't travel with you, Wes."

"Can't," he repeated, and sat up. "Why not?"

"My life is here. I really like my job and I don't want to leave it."

He nodded slowly as though considering. "I understand." He sent her a mischievous smile. "Doesn't mean I'm not going to use everything in my arsenal to change your mind."

Kaylee tried to smile.

His grin faded. "What else is going on? You don't seem yourself."

She stared out the window at the pines beyond. "Wes, what if I told you that I found out the doctors were wrong? About me not being able to get pregnant."

"I'd say that's amazing." He snorted. "And that you need to get on the pill, stat."

Her eyes narrowed and her mind suddenly went in another direction. "Not condoms?"

He looked at her innocently. "You ruined me. I must be inside you without anything between us."

"Are you serious right now?"

"No, I'd wear a condom," he grumbled. "But if it's all the same, I'd be happy for you to go on the pill."

She watched his eyes. "I'm not going on the pill... because I'm already pregnant."

His smile dropped. "Say again?"

She twisted her mouth and tapped her chin. "You know, you very well might have knocked me up that first night on the golf course. This is all your fault, if you think about it. You said you'd impregnated me, and you did. It's because of your cockiness and virility that we find ourselves in this situation."

He jumped off the bed. "What the fuck!" His stare was so intense that she thought he might have a heart attack.

"Sit down before you hurt yourself."

But he didn't sit. He walked around the bedroom, glancing every now and then at her stomach. "Can't be."

"It is."

"How?"

She gave him a look. "How do you think?"

"But you said..."

"I was wrong. The doctor who told me I couldn't get pregnant was wrong."

"But you've been...you know." He sighed. "I really don't like thinking of you with anyone else, so it pains me to bring this up, but you've been with others."

"I've been with *one* other since you. A person who can't have children." She lifted her eyebrow.

"Holy. Fuck." He started to pace again and ran his hand through his hair. He stopped to stare at her stomach, then shook his head and paced some more. And then he was muttering incoherently.

"Wes." He didn't acknowledge her. "Wes, you're starting to worry me."

He stopped at the edge of the bed, eyes wide, and swallowed. "Are you okay for a little while? Do you need anything?"

She shook her head slowly. She'd worried he would take the news badly, and this didn't look good.

"Okay. Because I need to see my brothers. But I'll be back." He glanced once more at her belly then left the room, keys in hand. She heard the front door open and close downstairs seconds later.

Was this how it was going to be? Zombie Wes? She

could handle Zombie Wes, because she was freaked out too. That wasn't what had her worried.

She was worried about ruining his dreams. The ones he'd finally grasped. And that he'd think she was ruining them too.

CHAPTER TWENTY-NINE

Wes sat at the bar in the Club Tahoe steakhouse. "I need to talk to you," he said to Bran, who was replacing a bottle on one of the glass shelves behind the bar.

"What's up?"

The place was dead, stuck between dining hours, but that wouldn't last long. Pretty soon, people would come pouring in for their gourmet dinner at one of the best restaurants in town. "It's personal," Wes said.

Bran set a bottle down, wiped his hands on a rag, and walked around the bar. He sat next to Wes. "You okay?"

Wes shook his head and took a deep breath. He'd believed Kaylee when she said she couldn't get pregnant—had beaten himself up over it, feeling responsible. And now, when everything was finally within grasp, she dropped this on him? "Kaylee just told me she's pregnant."

Bran's eyes widened. He ran a hand through his light hair and looked around as though he were just as shocked as Wes.

That wasn't what Wes needed. Dammit, he needed his

brother to be the coherent one. Because Wes thought he might be losing his mind.

Bran was the thinker—the one brother who didn't act without weighing all the consequences. He wouldn't have made love to a woman on the golf course without protection. Shit, Bran was such a monk these days, he wouldn't have made love to a woman on the golf course, period.

"You're not the first person to be a part of an unplanned pregnancy," Bran finally said. "I'm assuming it was unplanned?"

The only person Wes had told about the miscarriage Kaylee suffered was Bran. "Not planned."

"If I could go back in time, I know what I would have done if the girl I'd dated in high school had given me a choice. The question is, what do you want to do?"

Wes cut Bran a sharp look. "I want my kid. And I want to support Kaylee—no question. But there's more." He rubbed his forehead. "I just received word that I made it onto the tour for the rest of the year. The dream I've carried most of my life is coming true. But if I take this opportunity, I'd be gone almost all the time."

Bran shook his head. "Your timing leaves something to be desired."

Wes chuckled humorlessly. "Tell me about it. The problem is, I want it all. Kaylee, the baby—I even enjoy running the course now. I like teaching kids and training future stars at the game."

"But letting go of your dream, man...that's rough."

Wes glared. "Is that the best you've got? Didn't you used to be a bartender, listening to everyone's problems and shelling out advice?"

"Past tense." Bran stood and walked around the bar, picking up a clean glass. "Now I'm running four restaurants and would rather gouge my eyes out than listen to one more person's problems—brothers not included. I've got my fill of bullshit with these employees coming into work with all their issues." He filled the glass with amber liquid and sent it across the bar. "Liquid courage, brother. That's all I can offer. And not to put pressure on you or anything, but you've got one more problem. Levi's still worked up about you being gone. If you choose the tour, you'll need to find someone to help run the course. And that isn't what Dad would have wanted. Not that you need the reminder."

None of them, with the exception of maybe Adam, had been close to their father. But since their father's death, all of Wes's brothers had taken the responsibility of running the resort seriously, the way their father had dreamed. Like some sort of tribute to the old man.

Wes swigged the shot and pushed the glass across the counter. "Trust me, it hasn't slipped my mind."

Bran studied him as he poured Wes's next shot. "Kaylee's a good girl. You're different with her. Less tense. She make you happy?"

Wes nodded, but he wasn't ready to share his feelings about Kaylee with his brother when he hadn't shared them with her. He didn't want to hurt her, but this pregnancy? She could have slapped him across the face and he wouldn't have been more stunned.

Wes tipped back the second shot. "Better keep these coming. I'm going to need them while I sort this out."

———

KAYLEE WASN'T UPSET when Wes left her immediately after she'd told him about the baby. Honestly, she'd needed these last two days to come to grips with the idea too, and she was still in shock. But it was dark out now and Wes hadn't returned. And he'd not called or messaged her, either.

Prickly heat rose in her chest. She was sick of putting others' needs ahead of her own.

Kaylee had always felt like a cling-on to Wes's drive for glory in college. Even if she'd believed he loved her, it hadn't been enough. She'd wanted to be a priority. Then, when she was at her lowest, she'd met Eddy and he'd put her first. For a while. Until that was all a lie too. Eddy only loved himself. And here she was, hooking up with Wes again and pregnant, something she'd never thought possible.

Kaylee wasn't simply mad at Wes for running out and not checking back in. *She. Was. Pissed.*

She told him she was pregnant with their child, and he left her to huddle with his brothers? That asshole!

He was doing it again. Putting his needs ahead of hers. It had been coming on slowly with the golf tour, but she couldn't blame him for going for it and finally realizing his dreams. Only now she was pregnant and needed him too. Needed to talk it through with him, at the very least, and feel like she wasn't alone the way she'd been four years ago.

Would she never learn? She was alone.

Wes hadn't changed. And she couldn't even blame him for it. She'd slowly slipped into old habits too, not saying anything about the time he spent away, allowing him to show up whenever he felt like it. She'd told herself they weren't in a relationship to prevent this outcome. But they were. Kaylee wasn't seeing anyone else, and neither was Wes.

The only thing she couldn't understand was why he'd chosen to date her again. No matter how many times she'd told him she didn't want anything serious, he'd nod and keep right on wooing her into a relationship. He never said he loved her, though. Never talked about a future, unless it was one where she followed him around the country on the tour. And now she'd forced a future on him and he'd run.

Kaylee sank onto the couch and dropped her head in her hands. "Shit."

She wasn't even sure she'd be able to hold on to this pregnancy. She'd lost the first baby around the same time—which had ruined everything.

Kaylee stood and stormed into the kitchen. She shoved dishes into the dishwasher. Damn him! And what the hell was up with his sperm? How could he have gotten her pregnant the first time they had sex in four years? She didn't know if it had happened on the golf course, but it had to have occurred then or soon after, given how far along she was in her pregnancy. She shoved the dishwasher closed and crossed her arms—right as Wes walked through the front door.

His wide shoulders banged into the doorjamb. He nearly lost his balance completely when he tried to shut the door. She peeked out the window and saw a taxi pull away.

Kaylee narrowed her eyes. Even drunk, Wes was handsome. More so because he was off his guard, rumpled, sloppy, and boyish. "I tell you I'm pregnant, and you leave me to get hammered?"

He dumped his wallet on the coffee table, walked across the room, and sank onto the couch, lying back with his arm over his head. "Not now. Talk tomorrow?"

She stormed over and glared down at him. "Do you even want this baby?"

He moved his arm, revealing one steely eye. "You are not hurting our baby."

She threw up her arms. "Of course I'm not. God, Wes.

This could be the best thing that's ever happened to me. And I thought you'd at least be positive about it."

He covered his eye again. "I am."

"Yeah," she said. "You seem like it."

She locked the front door and turned back to him. He was snoring lightly, the jackass!

"Wes!" She went over and shoved his leg with her bare foot.

He jerked and seemed to try to sit upright, but instead flopped around on the couch. "What's wrong?" he slurred.

Everything. Simply everything.

She headed for the staircase. "Don't even try and get into my bed tonight or you'll find your drunk ass on the floor."

There. She'd told him.

But she hadn't really. Because Wes had gone out and gotten drunk, and not in the celebratory way. He'd gotten drunk in the "holy shit, my fuck buddy is pregnant, now what do I do" way.

Tears stung her eyes as she climbed the stairs. She'd be better off without him. A pain stabbed her in the chest and she rubbed it. Wes wasn't good for her or the baby. And no way was she losing *this* one.

Kaylee stood at the top of the stairs and cradled her tummy. "You and me first this time."

CHAPTER THIRTY

Wes left the next day for another tournament. He didn't need to be there for two days, but he'd needed the time to himself. Needed to figure out his next move. Because Kaylee had just turned his life upside down.

For once, he thought things couldn't be more perfect. He had Kaylee back in his life, and he'd just made the big time in golf. Okay, the lower end of the big time, given he wasn't winning tournaments, but still, shit was good.

With shaking hands, he dumped pain relievers into his palm and threw them back, along with a swig of water. His fucking head felt like he'd cracked it on the sidewalk. What the hell was in that whisky last night?

Then again, he'd lost track of how much he'd drunk after his fifth shot. That was probably his primary problem.

He'd played like crap during practice today and blamed it on the alcohol still leaching its way out of his system. But really, the reason could encompass any number of things—a beautiful brunette at the top of that list.

He had issues. Just because he was on the tour track, didn't mean everything was unicorns and rainbows. In the back of his mind, he'd been concerned about how to hold on to Kaylee while he traveled all the time. It wasn't a life most women would be happy with, and he'd already put Kaylee through hell years ago due to his golf ambitions. And now there was a baby to consider.

Jesus.

The tournament went much like his practice round. He'd played like crap and didn't make the cut, so he didn't earn anything. But that was fine, because his head wasn't in it. And when it came to golf, if your head wasn't in the game, you were screwed.

Wes flew back to Lake Tahoe and pulled into Kaylee's driveway no wiser than when he'd left, and a hell of a lot wearier. He shouldered on his travel bag and walked slowly up the steps to her parents' place. He reached for the front door, but it was locked.

Sighing, Wes bent and fumbled around for the hide-a-key, but it wasn't there either.

The fuck? He knocked on the front door. "Kaylee, open up."

Leaning his head against the door, he rested his dog-tired bones and listened for movement inside. She had to be here. Her car was in the driveway.

Finally, footsteps sounded on the other side of the door and he stepped back, relieved to be home and able to see his girl.

Home. Kaylee was his home.

She opened the door, but she wasn't smiling like she normally did when he returned from a tournament.

Fear gripped Wes's chest. Instinctively, he glanced at her stomach, not that he could tell if there was anything wrong by looking. "Is the baby okay?"

She leaned her shoulder against the doorjamb. Which

was odd. She'd not moved to let him in, and all he wanted was to hold her, maybe collapse on the couch and put his hand on her tummy. *Hmm,* never thought to do that before, but it sounded nice.

"It isn't a good idea for you to come inside," she said.

For a second, Wes's mind went blank. Why wouldn't he come in? They were going to have a baby. He'd not been able to verbally pin her down to a committed relationship, but as far as he was concerned, it was unspoken. He wasn't seeing anyone else, and she wasn't either.

Unless she was.

Jealousy gripped his chest, his face heating. "Why not?" The question came out harsher than he'd intended.

Kaylee swallowed and stood straight. "If this baby makes it..." Her voice was scratchy, and she blinked a couple of times. "I'll never keep you from visiting. I want you to be in the baby's life."

What was she talking about? It sounded like she was giving him the boot.

Not fucking happening.

Not again.

"Kaylee, I will be in this baby's life. I will be a father. Whatever you need."

She took a deep breath and a small smile crossed her lips, but it wasn't enough. Sadness lurked behind her eyes. "I'm happy to hear that."

Had she doubted it? "Let me in so we can talk."

She shook her head. "It's better this way. What we've been doing"—she waved between them—"it was never meant to last. I care so much about you, Wes, but it's time we end things and cut our losses."

He felt his jaw tense. For a split second, he'd thought

she'd moved on while he'd been gone, but that was a knee-jerk reaction. It wasn't like Kaylee to do that. Only it didn't matter in the end if she still pushed him away.

"No," he finally said.

She crossed her arms. "You don't have a choice. I told you I didn't want anything serious. Nothing's changed—"

"Everything's changed."

"—and I don't want us stuck in a relationship because I got pregnant. It's not right for either of us. And it's especially not right for the baby. He or she deserves parents who love each other."

It was on the tip of his tongue to tell her that he loved her. That he'd been fucked up these last few years because he loved her so damn much and losing her had messed with his head. But he didn't.

There was no doubt they were attracted to each other. The sheets went up in flames when they were together, but he didn't know if she loved him. And his pride took that moment to rear its head, preventing him from putting himself out there.

"Wes, we are right back where we left off. Golf is number one, and I'm... God, what am I to you? Number three? Four? What would the baby be to you?"

"I told you already. You're everything to me." It was the closest he could come to how he truly felt.

"But I'm not, don't you see? And I never will be. I don't want to take away your chance at the tour. You've done so well, and I care about you enough to want this for you. I promise I will never keep your child from you, if you want to be a part of his life."

"Her life."

"Her?"

"We're having a girl."

She sent him a confused look. "You don't know that."

He shrugged. "It's a hunch. Anyway, there's no way in hell I don't want to be a part of our daughter's life. Or yours." He leaned forward until their heads were mere inches apart. "You're mine, Kaylee."

———

KAYLEE COULDN'T IMAGINE LOVING anyone the way she loved Wes, so in some ways, he was right. She was his. And if everything went well, she was having his child. But she'd learned to put her needs first, and not simply set them aside so Wes could pursue his wants in life. The tour was *his* dream, not hers. And if she let him, he'd run over everything she held dear—friends, family, a job where she made a difference. Club Tahoe had given her back what she'd lost. She wasn't throwing it away for Wes's convenience.

And that was how she knew the two of them would never work out. She and Wes weren't going in the same direction, and he expected her to make all the compromises.

"Kaylee, I'm fucking tired as hell. I'm sorry for getting drunk after you told me about the baby, but don't make any decisions until we've had a chance to talk things out. And don't think I didn't notice you moved the hide-a-key. That thing has been there for over a decade." His tone turned dark. "I'll leave if it's really what you want. For now. But I'm coming back."

He turned and walked toward his car before she could tell him to not bother. A part of her wanted Wes in her life so badly... But that was the part she needed to ignore. Because that way only led to pain.

She blinked back tears. Her throat was dry from all the crying she'd done this week. He thought there was more to talk about, but there wasn't. She'd made up her mind.

Ending things was the right thing to do. It had to be. Now she just needed to live with it.

CHAPTER THIRTY-ONE

Kaylee wouldn't see him, and it was driving Wes insane. He'd gone by her house multiple times to talk to her, but she'd said the same thing each time—that it was over between them, but that she wouldn't keep their child from him. Not that he ever thought she would. That wasn't Kaylee. She was loving, and she'd always wanted what was best for children.

Fuck, she'd wanted what was best for him too. And he'd been a dick. He wasn't sure exactly how he'd managed it this time, but he was fairly certain he had.

Which made this entire situation so damn frustrating. Because what was right for him was being with her.

Levi, Emily, and Bran sat across from Wes in the Fireside Lounge, spearing him with blazing looks.

"You fucked up," Levi said.

Emily shook her head slowly. "If she leaves, Wes, so help me... You don't even want to know the kind of pain I will bring to your life."

Levi glanced pointedly at Emily, then back to Wes, as though saying, *Do you see what I mean?*

"Dude," Bran said, "fix it. Whatever you did, just fix it. Take it from me, you don't want to lose this chance."

Bran's words held weight, which might have slipped past Levi, but not Emily. Her gaze swung to Bran. "What do you mean, take it from you?"

Bran ducked and swigged his beer. "Nothing."

"I don't want to lose her," Wes said, helping Bran out. Bran obviously didn't want the others to know he'd gotten a girl pregnant in high school. For whatever reason, it seemed Wes was the only one he'd confided in. "I'm trying to make things right, but she's being stubborn as hell. Says we'll never work out. That it's just like before. But it isn't. I was an ass before, always thinking of myself, so caught up in my goals, I didn't know what was going on around me."

Levi raised an eyebrow. "You sure you're not doing the same thing?"

Was he? The tour wasn't his main priority, but his actions sure as hell made it so. And he'd not reacted right when she'd told him she was pregnant. In his defense, what man would under the circumstances?

But Levi might be onto something. Wes wasn't showing Kaylee all his cards, when she had just as much to lose as he did. If he wanted a chance with her, he needed to open up.

Wes hadn't fully told Kaylee how he felt about her. That he wanted to be with her. That he loved her... God, he could see them together forever. Which was damn scary if he considered it, but not as scary as losing her again. He wasn't sure how a person found their soul mate at the age of twenty, but he had.

Now he just needed to convince her of it.

CHAPTER THIRTY-TWO

The past few weeks, Kaylee sensed Wes making it a point of being around her more. Oh, he'd been traveling too, but the time between his tournaments stretched out longer and longer. He seemed to be waiting until the very last second before he had to be somewhere.

Not that it changed anything. She was moving on.

Okay, she wasn't really moving on. She missed him. But she had to think of the baby too. Kaylee was now fourteen weeks pregnant and past her first trimester. She wouldn't be comfortable until the baby was born healthy, but it was a relief to know she'd made it past the period when she'd lost their first child.

She told her parents about the baby, and her mother was ecstatic. The woman couldn't wait to be a grandmother. Her father, however, was furious and wanted to do bodily harm to Wes. Kaylee was unmarried, and her father still blamed Wes for getting her pregnant the *last* time. She couldn't fault his logic. It was only natural that her dad hadn't forgiven her ex-boyfriend/baby daddy.

Now that the shock of the pregnancy had worn off,

Kaylee was thrilled about the baby she never thought she'd be able to have. Wes was around, so that helped her not feel alone. In fact, he was beside her in the waiting room at her doctor's appointment. He'd insisted on going, and she saw no reason not to have him there.

Wes checked his watch. "They're late."

Kaylee dropped a hand to her small belly. She was starting to show a little. Goodbye, pants that fit. She could get away with looping a rubber band through the top buttonhole and hooking it to the button to give her extra space, but pretty soon she'd need to invest in maternity clothes. "Yep," she said calmly, flipping the page of a fashion magazine.

Ten minutes later, he checked his watch again. "Why aren't they calling us in?"

She turned to him, and he flinched. She might be giving him a death stare. "Do you want to be here or not?"

"Yes, I want to be here," he said. "But it's rude to make us wait... Isn't it?"

"Babies don't arrive when you tell them to. And my OB/GYN is very busy. She often has a long wait."

Wes stared at her. She could tell he was deciding how far to push it. He scratched his jaw. "As long as you're happy with the doctor." *Smart man.*

She smiled and settled back in her seat. "I am."

———

BY THE TIME the nurse called Kaylee's name, Wes had tipped his head back and taken a catnap. The doctor was forty-five minutes late, but Kaylee didn't seem to care, thus Wes didn't care. And that was what he'd realized. If Kaylee was happy, he was happy. Therefore, he slept.

But he was awake now. Due to Kaylee's history, they'd offered another ultrasound to give her peace of mind that the baby was all right. Wes was going to see his child for the first time, and he was ready to jump out of his skin.

His kid. With Kaylee. He was excited and terrified. What if something was wrong with the baby? What if Kaylee went through pain like she did with the miscarriage?

What was he thinking? Yes, she'd go through pain; childbirth was a bitch. Which was why he found himself in a perpetual state of anxiety.

They walked through the office to another room, where they waited fifteen more minutes—but who was counting—until the doctor came in.

"How is everyone doing?" she asked, closing the door behind her. Wes introduced himself, and she shook his hand.

"I'm feeling better," Kaylee said once the introductions had been made. "No more morning sickness."

"This is around the time when that typically goes away. You're taking the prenatals?"

Kaylee described the vitamins she was taking, and the doctor seemed pleased.

"Why don't we start with a measurement, and then we'll do the ultrasound."

Kaylee lay back on the examination table, and the doctor took out a measuring tape. She measured from Kaylee's pelvic bone to a spot above her belly button. "Your uterus is the size it should be for fourteen weeks. Let's take a look at the baby, shall we?"

The doctor oozed clear, goopy stuff on Kaylee's belly and brought out a wand. The images that popped up on the screen were a blur of shapes Wes couldn't decipher. He started to sweat, panic rushing through him. Was something wrong with the kid?

And then the doctor pressed a button and the sound of a fast-beating heart filled the room.

Kaylee's eyes glistened and she reached for his hand. It was the first time she'd let him touch her in weeks, and he didn't take the moment for granted. "That's our baby."

Wes breathed in nice and slow. There was no way he'd break down in the doctor's office over hearing his child's heartbeat. He could count on his hand the number of times since childhood that he'd felt close to tears, and almost all of them were since Kaylee had come into town. He'd become a sap, but he'd take it if it meant being with her. "That's really our daughter's heartbeat and not Kaylee's?"

The doctor smiled. "The child's heartbeat is much faster than the mother's. That's your baby, all right. Though I'm not sure if you have a *her*. Could be a boy. It's too soon to tell."

Kaylee wiped the corner of her eye and grinned. "Wes is certain it's a girl."

The doctor moved the wand around on Kaylee's belly. "The baby is in a good position. I could take a look, though any guess I make might not be accurate. Would you like me to try?"

"Yes," Wes said. He turned to Kaylee. "If it's okay with you?"

Kaylee nodded.

"Well," the doctor said after a moment of moving the wand in small increments, "I'm not seeing any little boy parts. It looks like Wes might be right, though we won't know for sure until around eighteen or twenty weeks."

Wes's ribcage expanded so much he thought his chest would explode. He was having a girl. He didn't care what the doctor said; he was certain. A little girl with the woman he loved...

Wes would make things right with Kaylee, no matter what it took. He had to prove to her that he would take care of her and their child and make them happy.

CHAPTER THIRTY-THREE

Wes had listened to his child's heartbeat, and then he was off to his next tournament. He almost didn't want to go.

More and more lately, Wes found himself glued to Kaylee's side, much to her confusion and annoyance. But dammit, he was desperate to be a part of Kaylee and their unborn child's life.

He found any excuse to swing by Club Kids, and brought Kaylee lunch every day he was in town, which she didn't seem to mind. Her appetite had expanded exponentially. If Wes got anywhere near her food, she gave him the evil eye.

Lesson learned: never come between a pregnant woman and her food if you value your limbs.

Halfway through his latest tournament, his buddy Tom invited him to go out for drinks. Wes wasn't big on drinking during a tournament, but Tom had insisted.

They'd just sat down at the bar and ordered beers when Tom started laying into Wes.

"I need a hookup." Tom scanned the bar, his gaze

landing on a short blonde in the corner. "Too tense out there on the course. Be my wingman tonight?"

Fuck. The last thing Wes wanted was to flirt with a woman so his friend could get laid. And why should he have to?

"Not tonight." *Or ever*, he thought.

Wes had a kid on the way. He wasn't in the same place as Tom anymore. Which was a shocking realization. He wasn't interested in the lifestyle his buddy led, and that Wes had led mere months ago, though even then he'd been getting tired of it.

Ever since Kaylee had come into town, Wes had stopped chasing women. He'd been training and busy, but really, it was like he'd become a compass needle pointed only at Kaylee. All else had faded into the background. She was the only woman he wanted, and it wasn't just about sex. Though he definitely wanted to have sex with her if she ever let him back in her bed.

Wes loved Kaylee. She was his equal—the woman he'd throw down for. The woman who told him he was being an ass when he was being an ass. And for some reason, a smackdown from Kaylee was worse than from anyone else.

He laughed when Emily, the velvet hammer, gave him a hard time, or when his brothers were up his ass. But if he upset Kaylee, he couldn't take it. He had to make things right as soon as possible, because the last thing he wanted was for her to be unhappy.

"No?" Tom said. He shook his head. "How quickly they forget. I got your golf course on the tour, which got you the sponsor's exemption. That's the only reason you're sitting here right now." He stared back at the blonde and the group of women she was with. "I think you owe me, don't you?"

Wes didn't mention that he'd played damn well, and

that was the reason he'd made it past the Tahoe Invitational. He sensed a threat when he heard one. "How long have you been a dick?"

Tom huffed out a breath. "Excuse me? You want to rethink your words? Don't forget, I'm in with the tour organizers. One word from me, and you'd get pulled just like that." He snapped his fingers.

Could he? Wes wasn't so sure, and he honestly didn't give a shit.

He rose from his chair and tossed down cash for his unfinished beer. "I'm heading back to the hotel. Enjoy your night."

Tom stood abruptly. "I won't forget this, you know," he called as Wes made his way to the exit.

Wes strode out of the bar where he hadn't wanted to be in the first place. And when he reached the hotel, he considered leaving the whole damn tournament. Which was insane. Or maybe not.

His brothers were right. It didn't matter how many sandwiches Wes brought Kaylee when he was in town. He was still gone most of the time. Which meant he was putting the tour ahead of his family with Kaylee, the same way his father had put the club ahead of Wes and his brothers.

He had a chance to be a real father, and what was he doing? Placing work ahead of the most important woman in his life and his future child just so he could dick around the pro tour circuit in the middle of the pack.

Could he qualify for the tour full-time? Win a tournament? Possibly. But then what would he have? Success would be hollow if he missed raising his daughter. And if he didn't have Kaylee.

Wes put in a few phone calls then packed his bags.

He knew where he wanted to be. And it wasn't here.

———

WHEN WES ARRIVED in Lake Tahoe, Kaylee wasn't home. He dropped his luggage off at his place and headed for the club. It was after hours, and he couldn't imagine where she might be, but he hoped one of his brothers would know before he ruined the surprise by calling her.

He didn't need to look far. And it wasn't one of his brothers who helped him out.

Wes walked into the Fireside Lounge and scanned the tables. Kaylee sat at the bar across from Emily, who was bartending, but only for Kaylee, it seemed. They were at one end of the bar, and the regular bartender was helping the rest of the customers at the other end.

Wes released a heavy sigh. Nothing like not knowing where the pregnant mother of your child was at nine o'clock at night. Not that it was late, but yeah, he just needed to know she was okay.

He started toward them, and Emily looked up. She held up her hand discreetly, staying him.

Kaylee took what appeared to be one of several orange shots, and Emily said something quietly in her ear. Kaylee nodded, and Emily hurried over to Wes.

Emily must not have told Kaylee that he stood in the lounge, because she didn't look back.

"What are you doing here?" Emily said in a hushed voice, glancing toward the bar.

"What am I doing here? Why are you giving my pregnant girlfriend shots of alcohol?"

"Girlfriend?" She quirked her eyebrow.

He sighed and motioned for her to continue. As far as Wes was concerned, Kaylee *was* his girlfriend.

"It's orange juice, not alcohol. Orange juice has folic acid in it, which is good for the baby."

Wes shook his head. "What the hell are you talking about?"

Emily grabbed his arm and dragged him out of the lounge and into the lobby. "Kaylee can't drink, but she didn't want to be alone tonight, so we're improvising. Now why are you here? Shouldn't you be on some golf course across the country?"

He glanced away. "I came back."

Concern crossed her face. "Did something happen?"

"Not exactly."

"Given how open you're being, I take it you're not going to tell me what's up?"

"Correct."

"Fine, but you can't be here right now." She peered toward the doorway of the Fireside Lounge, where they could just make out Kaylee lifting her next orange juice shot.

"Why the hell not?"

"Because Kaylee is feeling sad. It's not easy being a single pregnant lady."

"She doesn't have to be a single pregnant lady," he said. "I've been trying to show her that I want something serious."

"Well whatever you've been doing, it isn't working." She turned and started toward the lounge. "Maybe you should be more direct," she said over her shoulder, leaving him stammering.

Wasn't that what he was doing by leaving the pro tour to be with Kaylee?

Wes missed the club and his students, so leaving the tour wasn't only about her. He wanted to be there for his brothers as well. The truth was, he was happier in Lake Tahoe than on the road.

He'd been trailing Kaylee every chance he got when he was home, trying to show her he was there for her. But until today, the things he'd been doing were actions worked around his schedule.

Wes and Kaylee were adults with a child on the way. He needed to show her that he was serious and in it for the long haul.

Kaylee wanted direct? He'd show her direct.

CHAPTER THIRTY-FOUR

The next week, Wes put in forty hours at the club pro shop and golf course, making sure things were running smoothly. Bella came into town with her parents for the weekend, and he got in a couple of lessons with her as well. She was getting damn good. He couldn't wait to see where she'd be in a few years when she was a little taller. Even so, Bella had talent, and he got a rush out of helping her improve.

He got a rush helping all of the kids improve. Not the same kind of excitement he experienced on the tour, but maybe this was better. It wasn't all about him—the satisfaction he gained reached farther, touching more than just his life.

Bran walked up to the pro shop counter and leaned his arms against it. "You ready?"

Wes tucked away next week's schedule and grabbed his keys. "Yeah. You got the list from the broker?"

Bran patted his button-down's front pocket. "These should have what you're looking for. You were so fucking specific, the agent said there were only a couple of places that met your needs." He shook his head. "Why so many details?"

Wes nodded to his second in charge, indicating he was taking off, and came around the counter. "Actions, man. They're important."

"Actions?" Bran gave him a funny look. "Have you been drinking on the job?"

"No. Now come on, asshole. I've got a house to buy."

———

WES STARED at the bright pink walls of the children's bedroom. "Pepto-Bismol pink. This color won't do."

Bran shrugged. "The other house you liked had that one room with neutral kid colors."

"True, but this is the house. We'll just have to change the color in here."

The house they stood in was perfect, sitting in a cul-de-sac in a nice neighborhood, with wide lots, a three-car garage, and a large family room. The ideal place for his kid to play and make a mess of things.

Growing up, Wes lived in a mansion, and his father liked to keep it in perfect order for when his business associates came into town. They had a huge yard for Wes and his brothers to play in, but the house itself was off-limits for grimy little boy fingers. Wes wanted a home his kid could roam and feel comfortable in.

"I'm going to make an offer on it."

Bran looked around. "You sure this is what Kaylee wants?"

"No. But it's the gesture that counts, right?"

"I don't know." Bran shook his head slowly. "Don't women like to pick out their homes?"

How should Wes know? He'd never cared what a woman thought. Except for Kaylee. And he hoped like hell she'd like the place he chose for her.

He had been picky, insisting on a house close to the club, but far enough away for privacy and a natural landscape. The place also had to be well built and big enough for a family. And it needed to be in a nice, safe neighborhood for his kid. Which meant it cost a fortune. But Wes could afford it, especially after he'd pulled in decent earnings from the tour. But those weren't the only reasons he liked this place.

This home had a bright kitchen with a dining nook and tall windows that looked out onto the forest beyond. Kaylee had always loved that about her parents' place, and he hoped this house would make her happy too. With four bedrooms, three baths, and an office, there'd be plenty of space for her and their daughter. Or all of them, if Kaylee let him be a bigger part of her life.

He hoped he'd be included, but no matter what, this house was hers to do with what she wanted. She could sell it and find something else, or live in it forever. Either way, he would have it put in her name.

Wes smacked his brother's chest with the back of his hand. "Come on. Let's go make an offer."

CHAPTER THIRTY-FIVE

Wes held up two paintbrushes. "Well? What do you think?" he asked his brothers, plus Jaeg, who'd been recruited for his woodworking skills. They were all piled in the small bedroom of the new home. It closed yesterday, two weeks after Wes had made a cash offer. Technically, the room they stood in wasn't small, but with six strapping men inside, the place filled up fast. "Light green or lavender?"

"Green," Levi said. "No way you can know it's a girl. Green's more versatile."

"Fuck you. I know." Wes looked to Adam. "What do you think?"

Adam tilted his head and scratched his neck. "Both?"

Wes looked at the paintbrushes. "That's not a bad idea. Do we go half up the wall with one color, add a chair rail, then paint the top half with the other color?"

"You mean, will I add the chair rail?" Jaeg said.

"You think I know how to do that shit?"

Jaeg stretched his large arms over his head, briefly

touching the eight-foot ceiling. "Just making sure I know my duties here."

"Manual labor," Bran said. "That's what we're good for."

"Or," Wes said, ignoring the jackasses, "we could paint an accent wall."

Adam looked up from his phone, pausing in what Wes assumed was a text to Hayden. "Since when do you know about accent walls? I didn't know you'd turned into Martha Stewart."

"Fuck you, asshole." Wes set the paintbrushes back in the trays. "I've been poring over design magazines and talking to people. Thank God I'm only doing one room." He brushed his hands on his work jeans. "Executive decision time. Jaeg will build the chair rail and we'll do half up and half down, green on the bottom. Then Levi can use his manly muscles and put up the delicate girly decals on the walls."

Levi bit into a sandwich. "On it."

Jaeg cut the wood for the chair rails in the large garage, where Wes had set up a work space equipped with a fridge full of beers and snacks, and Wes put together part of the crib while the rest of the guys painted the bedroom.

Wes wasn't sure the finished crib would fit through all the doorways, so he set up the sides while he waited. He would finish putting the crib together once the walls were painted in the baby's room. The rest of the furniture he'd bought local and came already assembled.

Emily had helped him out with some of the other items she thought Kaylee might need in the nursery, like a rocking chair and an ottoman and a diaper pail. And about a million other little things Wes had no idea what to do with. He'd shoved them in the closet for Kaylee to organize later.

If she liked the house.

God, he hoped she liked it.

With six strong guys—one of them actually skilled at construction—the room was ready in a few hours. Now it was time to visit Kaylee.

Wes hadn't been around Kaylee as much as he would have liked these last couple of weeks, but he'd still made sure to bring her lunch every day and check in on her.

Okay, he walked by Club Kids about six times a day, but who was counting? Weekends were torture. He could only get away with checking in on her once or twice, though work and preparing the new house had kept him busy.

Kaylee was already asking him questions he couldn't answer. About the tour and why he'd been home these last few weeks. He didn't want her to think he was giving up his dream for her. She'd feel guilty, and she'd worry. So he'd waited until he could explain things properly. And the time had come.

Wes drove home, cleaned up, and went to Kaylee's parents' house. He and the guys had gotten started early this morning, so it was only six in the evening by the time Wes rolled up to her place.

He knocked on the front door and waited. And shifted his feet. And waited some more. Kaylee was almost halfway through her pregnancy and was getting slower. Or Wes was impatient. Mostly, he was impatient.

The door swung open, and there she was. Sweatpants, small ponytail on the top of her head, holding up only half of her hair because the rest was too short, with yellow gloves on her hands. "Wes? Is something wrong? I wasn't expecting you."

He glanced at the giant yellow rubber gloves. "I can see that."

"Oh." She stepped inside, pulled off the gloves, and set them on the kitchen counter. "Sorry. I was scrubbing the floor."

Wes frowned. "You shouldn't be doing that. I'll hire someone to clean the place."

She rolled her eyes. "I'm pregnant, not incapacitated. Besides, I've got strong nesting instincts going on right now. I need the release."

Wes's mind went straight to other forms of release, which he quickly shut down. Not the time. Hopefully, if he was a lucky son of a bitch, there would be. Until then, he'd used his memory bank of naked Kaylee images to pleasure himself. It was like high school all over.

"I've cleaned this entire house, top to bottom," Kaylee said, cutting into Wes's sexual musings. "Just need to decide which room to make into the baby's."

On that note... "I came by because I wanted to show you something. Do you have time?"

"Sure, when?"

"Now?"

She stared down at her outfit. "Not sure I'm fit to go out in public."

He looked at her stomach, swollen with their child. Her cheeks were flushed from the activity she'd been doing, and she wore no makeup.

He swallowed, overwhelmed by all he felt for this woman. "You're beautiful."

Kaylee smiled slightly, her expression soft but curious. "Give me a sec."

She wobbled slightly as she hurried into the kitchen and washed her hands. She pulled the small ponytail from her hair and smoothed down the dark strands, then slipped on a pair of flip-flops. "I hope this is okay, because it's about as good as it gets for me today."

____

CHAPTER THIRTY-SIX

Wes had never been more nervous in his life. And that included the time he'd played in his first professional golf tournament.

What if Kaylee hated the house? Or the nursery? What the fuck did he know about decorating?

He focused on the road and tried to not think about all the reasons this could go badly. But he had to give it a shot. Had to show Kaylee how much she meant to him. This wasn't only about the baby. It was about grabbing his second chance at being with the woman he'd always loved and had never gotten over.

He pulled into the driveway of the three-thousand-square-foot house that boasted rustic accents, like many of the newer homes in Lake Tahoe. The place carried a mountain vibe, with a triangular vestibule and log accents, but it didn't look like the club's version of mountain chic. Which was good, because he wanted Kaylee to feel like she was home and not at work.

Kaylee glanced around as Wes got out of the Range

Rover and walked over to the passenger side. "Where are we?"

He helped her out of the car and closed the door, shoving a nervous hand in his pocket. "We're at the house I bought you."

Her head slowly turned to him. "What?"

Was that a good what? A bad what? *Fuck.*

"Your house. I bought you a house with the money I earned on the tour. I still have the trust my father gave me, and I'm hoping you can help me figure out how best to spend it. Or save it, if we want to save it for our daughter." He rubbed his mouth. "I don't know."

"Whoa." She held up her hands. "Slow down. No, actually, back up. You bought me a house?"

He nodded. "For you and our daughter."

"Or son."

"Whatever." But it was a girl. And he was pretty damned ecstatic about it too. Ever since they dated in college, he'd wanted a daughter who looked like Kaylee.

She waved her hands in a halting manner. "Why did you buy me a house?"

Wes faced her and grabbed her hands. They were unsteady, and he squeezed them reassuringly. "I want to provide for you and our child. I want you to feel safe and important. And I want to love you. This is how I show my love. Not by buying you something extravagant, but by taking care of the two most important people in my life: you and our daughter."

"Or son," she said dazedly. "Love. You said *love.*"

"I love you. I've always loved you. I only said I was fine with a casual relationship because I didn't want to scare you away. But then I knocked you up with my powerful sperm" —she smiled—"and I had some figuring out to do. I thought I could take the opportunity I'd been given with the tour as long as I spent my off time with you. But I couldn't have both."

"Wes," she said, "I didn't want you to have to choose."

"I know that. Which is why I needed to figure it out on my own. And you know what? Fuck the tour. Success is empty if you're not there at my side. You deserve to be happy and not waiting around for me to show up after I'm done doing my thing."

He pulled her close and felt her pregnant belly tuck up against him. "To be honest, the tour got old. There was a moment when I realized I wasn't even happy. I love golf, and who doesn't want to be a star on the tour? But nothing makes me happier than being with you."

A tear escaped her eye and she swiped it away. "That was beautiful." She waved her hand at the house. "This is beautiful. But I'm still worried you'll regret letting go of your dream."

Of course she was. She wouldn't be Kaylee if she didn't worry about that.

He nodded. "Come on. Let's go inside. I have something else to show you."

Wes opened the front door, and Kaylee gasped. "The windows."

The front opened up to the kitchen, which was highlighted by those tall glass windows Wes thought Kaylee would like. "I chose this house because of the kitchen and the view. It reminded me of you."

She pressed her lips together. More tears ran down her cheeks. "Nope. Not budging. Sticking to my guns," she mumbled. "Gotta take care of the baby."

She seemed to be talking to herself. Was this some sort of pregnancy thing?

They walked through the house and Kaylee oohed and aahed, which was a relief. And then Wes took her upstairs to the bedrooms.

They walked down the hallway, and he showed her the spare bedroom and the master. Kaylee walked onto the deck off the master suite and breathed in the pine-scented air. "You have good taste, Wes."

He smirked. "I certainly do. I chose you." She gave him a look, and he laughed. "Come on. There's one more bedroom I want you to see."

After the guys had left and Wes had cleaned up, he'd closed the bedroom door to the nursery, leaving the window open to air out the fresh paint scent. He didn't want the surprise to come too soon when he showed up at the house with Kaylee.

Wes paused at the door, nervous as hell. What if the room was ugly? God, he should have hired a professional. But then it wouldn't have meant as much.

He held his breath and stepped back, opening the door for her.

Kaylee's mouth parted, but she didn't say anything, simply gazed around the room with wide eyes. Was that a good sign?

"Damn you." More tears streamed down her face. But she'd been doing that a lot lately. He couldn't tell if they were good or bad tears, but he hoped like hell they were the good kind.

"Does that mean you like it?"

She turned to him and swallowed. "I love it. This room is the most beautiful thing I've ever seen."

It really wasn't. The room was light green and lavender, with rustic-looking baby furniture and colorful forest fairy decals. But he figured once Kaylee rearranged things and made it homey, it would be nice for their daughter. He just wanted it to be set up for when the baby came. And to show Kaylee how much he loved her and their child. "You sure you like it?"

She turned and wrapped her arms around him, her head tucked to his chest. "I love it."

"You think you'd want to live here?"

Her head bobbed up and down. "You'll have to drag me away tonight."

He grinned. "Good. Because I have one more surprise."

"You've already given me so much."

"Not everything. Go look inside the crib."

Kaylee walked over and Wes followed, his heart hammering in his chest.

He heard her gasp. "Wes..." She reached down to the small pillow at the top of the crib. Apparently, baby bedding was supposed to be minimal, so there wasn't much except a sheet and this thing called a bumper. But Wes had bought a small pillow for his last surprise.

She picked up the dark blue jewelry box and opened it. More tears spilled from her eyes and her nose turned rosy. He wanted to lean over and kiss it, but he had a job to do.

Wes dropped to one knee. "Kaylee Isabelle Evans, I've loved you from the moment I saw you at a shady fraternity party in college. People say there's no such thing as love at first sight, but that's what it was. I thought we'd spend the rest of our lives together. And then I screwed up. And life took a turn neither of us was ready for. But my heart never moved on. It was always with you.

"I want to love you and our children, and share a life together. And I don't want to be away from you ever again. That's the reason I left the tour. It wasn't worth losing everything I love. And in the end, the tour didn't make me happy—you do. So please put my brothers and everyone else who's had to interact with me since you've been gone out of their misery. Say you'll marry me."

She smiled. A watery smile that was the most brilliant thing he'd ever seen. "Yes."

"Yes?"

"Yes."

Wes stood and picked her up with his arms beneath her knees and back, and carried her to the open window. "She said yes!" he yelled to the world.

And then he was kissing her, and it was like the Sahara Desert receiving a drop of rain.

God, she tasted good. Her lips, her body against his. Before he knew it, they were both kneeling on the ground and grabbing at each other.

"I'm so horny," she said between kisses.

It had been a century since they'd had sex. He practically had blisters on his hand from taking care of himself, but he didn't want to get his hopes up in her delicate condition. "Oh?" he said casually, returning every kiss she offered.

"Yes," she said breathily. "These darn pregnancy hormones are driving me crazy. Do you think it's too soon to...you know?"

God no. "Are you saying you want an orgasm, Kaylee?" he said, low and sultry.

Her face turned bright red. "Yes."

"I can provide that." Wes kicked off his shoes and tore off his shirt, pants, and underwear.

Kaylee was laughing and holding her belly. "I guess I didn't need to ask."

"You have no idea. I've been blue-balling it for weeks."

He grabbed her bottom and pulled her close. "But do you think we should christen *this* particular room?"

He kissed her neck and slipped off her top, just trying to save time. If he needed to, he could pick her up and carry her elsewhere, but he might as well get the disrobing done without wasting precious seconds deciding.

"The baby will never know. And besides, it's why we're here in the first place."

Wes stopped kissing her and held her face gently in his hands. "We're here because I found you again. Baby or not, I would have made you mine."

She kissed him on the lips, a soft, delicate touch that sent a flame to his groin. "Maybe you should pull off my pants."

"Sexiest words I've ever heard."

Kaylee stood, and Wes pulled off her sweatpants as instructed. And then he was on his back and Kaylee was on top of him, easing onto his body.

Wes let out a slow breath. Better keep it together or this would be very short.

He was trying to unhook her bra to get a view of her beautiful pregnancy boobs when her first orgasm hit. Her hips continued to undulate on him. "Oh, God," she said seconds later. "Another is coming."

Her pace picked up and Wes shoved up her bra, touching her and holding on. By the second orgasm, he was right there with her, filling her and cherishing her and so fucking thankful.

When they'd both caught their breath, he helped ease her onto her side next to him and held her close, staring into her eyes. "Maybe we should get you knocked up more often. Pregnancy sex is the best sex ever."

"Ever?"

"Okay, not ever. Every time is amazing. But just think of the number of orgasms you could have had if I hadn't been ready to explode. I think we need to investigate this theory. Like, how many can you accomplish while you're riding the hormone rollercoaster?"

She laughed.

"You don't think I'm serious?" He leaned over and kissed her neck. "Because I am. Mission Multiple Orgasms for Kaylee is so on."

CHAPTER THIRTY-SEVEN

When Kaylee had asked Wes what kind of wedding he wanted, he'd requested something small, but had left it up to her. Truthfully, Kaylee wasn't interested in anything elaborate either. That was how they ended up at the Chapel of the Twin Pines in South Lake Tahoe with her mother, a less angry father, now that Wes had made her "a respectable woman," and Wes's four brothers. Along with one wife, one girlfriend, and a retired secretary of Club Tahoe who was more of a part of the family to Wes and his brothers.

Hunt caught the bouquet *and* the garter, then proceeded to flirt shamelessly with the only single woman in the room—the fifty-dollar photographer they'd paid to capture their magical moment.

At some point during the wedding, Hunt had disappeared, presumably with the photographer. Bran, Adam, and Levi had started drinking heavily from silver flasks Kaylee was suspicious of, and her father had started singing "Bella Maria." Apparently, Wes had given her father his own flask, and her conservative dad had taken the opportunity to imbibe at his only child's wedding.

It was the most crazy, romantic, beautiful wedding, and it had been perfect.

Esther, their former secretary and close family friend, walked up to Wes and gave him a big squeeze. "I'm so happy for you, dear." She pulled out an envelope. "Just one small thing from your father."

"My father?" He looked confused.

"He wanted you to have it when the time was right," Esther said. "Asked me to wait until you'd fallen in love."

"My dad, Ethan Cade, talked about love?"

She grinned. "Yes, he did."

Wes shook his head. "Okay." He opened the envelope and read the letter.

Tears filled his eyes. "Fuck."

"Is everything okay?" Kaylee asked.

"Fine. Just my father pulling at the heartstrings from the grave." He handed her the letter.

Dear Wes,

You're my most competitive son, and I love you for it. Reminds me of myself. But damn if you're not a stubborn man. Also something you might have inherited from me.

I wasn't the best father. Put the club ahead of you boys. I didn't realize how terrible of a father I was until it was too late. Treat your wife well, cherish her, and know that I always loved you and your brothers, even if I didn't show it. In fact, learn from my mistakes and don't do that with your own children.

I have no doubt you'll make a great parent. It's a challenge, after all, and you never could pass one up.

Love,
Dad

KAYLEE REACHED over and gave him a hug. "He loved you."

"It would seem so."

"Did you really not know?"

"I knew, but you read the letter. He wasn't great at showing it." He looked into her eyes. "He's right about one thing, though. I'll always put you and our children first."

She cupped his jaw. "I don't doubt it anymore. I know you will."

"Well, I'm off," Esther said, breaking the heavy mood. "I have a date with a wealthy retiree."

Wes shook his head. "Esther, you're like a second mom to me. Please don't share these things. You dating gives me disturbing visuals."

She chuckled and kissed him on the cheek, then gave Kaylee a hug. "Be happy."

"We will," Kaylee said.

They watched Esther saunter out, charming the group as she went.

Wes caught Kaylee's eye and slipped his arm around her ever-expanding waist now that she was six months along. "*Are* you happy?"

She smiled at him. "Very."

He looked around. At her father still singing in the middle of the room while her mother covered her eyes. At the guys drinking in the corner. And at the plastic bouquets decorating the "chapel." "It was a rather charming wedding.

We couldn't have done better. But I insist on a kickass honeymoon."

"You mean babymoon. This belly goes where I go."

He leaned down and nuzzled her ear. "The belly is the best part. Do I need to remind you, *six* orgasms? I'm shooting for seven."

Kaylee felt her face flush. Wes had been serious with his multiple orgasms research. Never had a man been more determined, and boy did she reap the benefits. "Okay, but only if you insist."

"I do." A mischievous look came over his face. "And I say we start now."

Kaylee found herself slipping out the back alley of the Chapel of the Twin Pines in the arms of her husband, laughing as he cursed the width of the back door while he wielded his growing wife through it. They made it back to their house to christen another bedroom before the rest of the wedding party showed up.

And Wes beat his orgasm goal, making his wife a very, very happy woman.

Who would have thought Club Tahoe could have survived under Bran and his brothers' ownership for an entire year? Certainly not Bran, but here he was, making his way toward the anniversary party in a room at the back of the resort.

He strode through the hallway and shook his head, looking down—and nearly ran into Ireland, Cali's cousin.

"Oh, Bran... I'm so sorry. I wasn't looking where I was going."

Unless she'd been looking down as well, no one was *that* blind.

She wore a long navy gown that accented her porcelain skin. Against his will, Bran's gaze dipped. Ireland's red hair fell in waves across her forehead and neck and grazed the edges of her breasts. Breasts that must have filled a push-up bra to maximum capacity, and currently threatened to fall out of her dress.

His brothers liked to call him a monk, but Bran was a man—*he looked*. He also knew fake boobs when he saw them.

Ireland was the type of woman Bran had avoided for nearly ten years. Fast, seductive—and shallow. He could spot her kind a mile away.

"No problem." He moved to walk past her, and her hand fell lightly on his arm.

She'd been sending him looks ever since they'd met months ago, and he wanted none of it. Bran pulled his arm away.

"Have I done something to offend you?" She sounded hurt.

Sure he'd hurt her—her pride, that was. No way a woman as attractive as Ireland had suffered a day in her life. She'd take his rejection and move on to the next guy.

"No." He strode away and entered the party, sighing in relief. Another catastrophe averted.

Bran's brothers thought he didn't date. They were wrong. He liked women as much as his hound-dog brothers; he simply chose different women. He didn't date the ladies who came on to him at bars. And he didn't date flashy, beautiful women. The end.

Beautiful women were trouble, and deep down, he was still weak where they were concerned. Which was why he did everything he could to avoid them and live by the rules he'd set.

Inside the party was in full effect, with Bran's buddy Jaeg standing near the door with his fiancée Cali.

Jaeg stepped forward and shook Bran's hand. "Way to go, man. I figured you guys would have thrown in the towel six months ago and hired a management company."

"You and everyone else," Bran said. "But we're rolling with it. For now. We'll see how the next year goes." He leaned over and gave Cali a hug.

She returned the greeting, but her gaze scanned past his shoulder. "Have you seen my cousin?"

Bran's eye twitched. "We ran into each other in the hallway."

Jaeg chuckled. "Her vision isn't the—"

Cali elbowed Jaeg in the ribs, and he flinched.

Goddamn funny to see these two together. Jaeg was the tallest of Bran's friends, at six foot six, and his girlfriend was short. Or maybe she was average height, but she looked short next to Jaeg. Yet Jaeg was a pile of dough in her hands.

Jaeg sent Cali a look, and she returned it. "Ireland is a little clumsy, that's all," Cali said. "She's still new in town and I want to make sure she's having a nice time. She seemed off when she left for the restroom."

Bran glanced at the crowd. "Ireland appears social. I can't imagine her having a hard time making friends." *Understatement.* That woman knew what she was doing, running into Bran in the hallway like that. And shooting him interested glances every chance she got.

Yeah, she was one to avoid.

"Oh good," Cali said brightly. "I'm schooling her."

"Schooling her?"

Jaeg groaned. "Cali thinks Ireland needs more excitement in her life."

"Well, she does," Cali said.

"Babe, do you remember how this worked out the last time you helped a friend meet men?"

"This is totally different. Ireland is somewhat shy, and she's been working multiple jobs finishing her degrees; she's not had the opportunity to meet many people. Not fun people, anyway. That's what we're working on."

Bran caught the eye of the waitress he'd been casually

talking to for months. She quickly glanced away. Now *that* woman was shy. And just his type. He didn't need or want aggressive women. "Will you excuse me? I see someone I want to say hello to."

"We'll catch you later," Jaeg said, as Cali continued to talk about Ireland.

Bran tuned it out and made his way to the kind waitress. He'd not wanted to hear anymore about Ireland the "clumsy" redhead. The waitress he'd been talking to was pretty and sweet. She wouldn't complicate his life. Of course, Bran hadn't made a move there yet. Hadn't mustered up the energy to ask her out. Which was how he knew she was safe. His brain didn't cloud over when he saw her, and his libido was never in control.

His desires would never rule over him again.

———

I hope you enjoyed *Daring Wes*!

Sign up for my newsletter to receive monthly writing updates and new release emails. You'll also gain access to the Subscriber Extras page on my website that includes free extra scenes. Scan the QR code below:

Want to know what's going on inside that handsome head of Bran's? Grab *Seducing Bran* now.

xoxo,

Jules

SEDUCING BRAN

The wrong brother…

Ireland needs a fresh start, and her cousin convinces her to take a chance on a charismatic bad-boy with a wicked boat and a killer body. But when Ireland shows up for the popular Lake Tahoe booze cruise he runs, she finds his handsome older brother at the helm instead.

Bran likes things structured and predictable. Especially after the mistakes he made ten years ago. But his father's recent passing threw his calm life into chaos, and now Bran is in charge of the family's five-star restaurants. He's been grasping to get things back to status-quo ever since.

He has no idea how much more complicated life will get.

Flame-haired Ireland is exactly the type of beautiful woman Bran has programed himself to avoid. But when she falls into his lap on a booze cruise his brother asked him to cover, the boat isn't the only thing tossed by the water. Bran's heart goes overboard as well.

Headstrong Ireland is nothing Bran wants, and everything he needs.

Grab *SEDUCING BRAN* Now!

ABOUT THE AUTHOR

Jules Barnard is a *USA Today* bestselling author of romantic comedy and romantic fantasy. Her romantic comedies include the All's Fair, Never Date, and Cade Brothers series. She also writes romantic fantasy under J. Barnard in the Halven Rising series *Library Journal* calls "...an exciting new fantasy adventure." Whether she's writing about steamy men in Lake Tahoe or a Fae world embedded in a college campus, Jules spins addictive stories filled with heart and humor.

When she isn't in her sweatpants writing and rewarding herself with chocolate, Jules spends her time with her husband and two children in their small hometown in the Pacific Northwest. She credits herself with the ability to read while running on the treadmill or burning dinner.

www.julesbarnardbooks.com